STRIKEOUT OF THE BLEACHER WEENIES

AND OTHER WARPED AND CREEPY TALES

STRIKEOUT OF THE BLEACHER WEENIES

AND OTHER WARPED AND CREEPY TALES

DAVID LUBAR

A TOM DOHERTY ASSOCIATES BOOK
NEW YORK

STRIKEOUT OF THE BLEACHER WEENIES
AND OTHER WARPED AND CREEPY TALES

Copyright © 2016 by David Lubar

Reader's Guide copyright © 2016 by Tor Books

"Abra-ca-Deborah" originally appeared in *Dreams and Visions: Fourteen Flights of Fantasy,* edited by M. Jerry Weiss and Helen S. Weiss. Story © 2007 by David Lubar

All rights reserved.

A Starscape Book
Published by Tom Doherty Associates
175 Fifth Avenue
New York, NY 10010

www.tor-forge.com

The Library of Congress Cataloging-in-Publication Data is available upon request.

ISBN 978-0-7653-7726-5 (hardcover)
ISBN 978-1-4668-5463-5 (e-book)

Our books may be purchased in bulk for promotional, educational, or business use. Please contact your local bookseller or the Macmillan Corporate and Premium Sales Department at 1-800-221-7945, extension 5442, or by e-mail at MacmillanSpecialMarkets@macmillan.com.

First Edition: September 2016

Printed in the United States of America

0 9 8 7 6 5 4 3 2 1

For Tom Doherty, a smart man with a big heart.
Thank you for starting it all, and for supporting the work
and nurturing the careers of so many writers.

CONTENTS

CONTENTS

STRIKEOUT OF THE
BLEACHER
WEENIES

AND OTHER WARPED AND CREEPY TALES

EASY TARGETS

From the instant I heard about PeaceJoy Charter School, I knew I had to go there. I'd spotted a big article about it in the newspaper my parents were reading at breakfast. There was a headline on the front page of the local section: BULLY-FREE SCHOOL SET TO OPEN IN SEPTEMBER.

Wow. A school without any bullies. According to the article, students from anywhere in the city or the surrounding suburbs could apply to go there. I closed my eyes and pictured it. I smiled as I saw smart, unathletic kids walking safely and happily through hallways decorated with inspiring posters about working together and being friends with everyone.

Imagine that—a school without a single bully.

Better yet—imagine a school with just one bully: Me. All those pathetic little losers would be at my mercy. They say bullies feel bad about themselves. Not me. I feel great. I'm strong and powerful. And I'm smart. Smart enough not to get caught. Smart enough, at times, so that even my victim doesn't realize he's being bullied.

Yeah, that's how good I am at making little whiny rodents

11

feel fear and misery. I can make them tremble, blink back tears, and look in vain desperation for an escape route. But, as good as I am, nobody is perfect. I'd coasted through sixth and seventh grades without getting caught, but some of the teachers at my middle school had started to look at me like they were suspicious. When I walked through crowded hallways between classes, most kids tried to avoid getting too close to me. I had a feeling I'd end up in trouble before I finished eighth grade. I was afraid that my reputation for being a troublemaker would follow me to the high school, which was right across the street. So, it was time for a change, and for new hunting grounds.

I'd convinced my parents to fill out an application to Peace-Joy. That was easy enough. They aren't all that smart. Sometimes, I wonder where I came from. Maybe I had a great-great grandparent who was related to some brutal warlord or military genius. I sure didn't share any traits with my parents. I could twist them both around my little finger. They'd do anything I asked.

I had to write an essay as part of the admissions process for the school. That was a joke. I knew exactly what they wanted to hear. I tossed in phrases like "tired of being picked on," "peer pressure," and "self-esteem," and capped it all off with "I just want to be allowed to learn at my own pace in a fear-free and nurturing environment." It was priceless. I laughed the whole time I was writing it.

I got accepted, of course. The letter from PeaceJoy came two weeks before school started. I would be a member of the first graduating class. I'd walk the halls along with fifty-nine other students drawn from sixteen different middle schools in this part of the state.

I couldn't wait.

My dad dropped me off in front of the school the first morning.

"I'm proud of you, son," he said. "It takes a real man to admit his weaknesses."

"And strengths," I said as he drove off.

I merged with a group of kids going up the steps, and looked around, wondering who would be my favorite target this year. Maybe I could trip someone on the stairs. That was always fun. But it might be smarter to wait until I had a better sense of my classmates.

"Hey!"

I went tumbling.

Someone had tripped me.

I looked around as I got up, but I couldn't tell who had done it. It had to be an accident. Nobody here would dare do that on purpose.

I went in through the doorway.

"Hey!" I shouted again as someone smacked the back of my head. I looked around. Once again, I couldn't tell anything. But as I took a good look at the kids near me, I realized something disturbing.

I wasn't towering over the crowd.

This wasn't the way I'd pictured things. This wasn't the fantasy that had entertained me ever since I'd learned about PeaceJoy. Most of the other kids were my size . . . or bigger. There were one or two runts, but they didn't look scared. Their expressions were tough. They seemed alert, like they were looking all around for any source of danger. Or maybe they were looking for targets.

The teachers, who were waiting inside, led us into the auditorium. I got hit twice more before I took a seat. I sat in the last row, so there'd be nobody behind me. I noticed a banner over the stage:

PEACEJOY CHARTER SCHOOL: MAKING SCHOOLS SAFER EVERY-WHERE

Everywhere? That didn't make sense.

A huge kid sat on my left. He was so big, at first I thought he was a teacher.

"Give me your lunch money," he said.

I didn't even try to argue. That's how scary he was. Right after I handed over my money, the kid on my right said, "Give me your sneakers."

He was even bigger.

I looked around the auditorium, wondering who I could steal lunch money and sneakers from. That's when it hit me—and it hit me so hard, I almost threw up. I wasn't the only kid who realized it would be great to be the one bully in a school full of victims.

Everyone had that idea. Every bully in sixteen different schools. And, based on the banner, the people who ran Peace-Joy already knew it. They were making schools safer by stuffing all of us here. Other schools would be safer. But not this one, for sure.

It was going to be a rough year.

PARASITES

There's a poem my grandmother taught me:

Little bugs have lesser bugs
Upon their backs to bite 'em.
And lesser bugs have smaller bugs,
And so on, ad infinitum.

Being as I was a young lad when I first heard this, she had to explain to me that "ad infinitum" meant infinitely. And, of course, she then had to explain what "infinite" meant. But I understood the basic idea that the small bugs that bit people had their own smaller bugs that bit the people-biting bugs. And those smaller bugs had even smaller bugs to deal with. And so on.

It seemed fair.

I mention bugs because the place we moved to isn't all that clean. The bugs don't really bother me. But it's hard not to notice them as they scurry in the shadows or dart beneath the cabinets.

On the bright side, the people around us are interesting. From the start, I could tell it was a lively neighborhood, filled with the scents of exotic, spiced foods and the sounds of rhythmic, pulsing music. One person, in particular, caught my eye. Her name was Lolana. Pretty name. Pretty girl.

She noticed me, too. The first day there, when I was walking to school, I could tell that I'd caught her attention as I moved past the stoop where she and her friends were gathered— waiting, I assume, for the last possible minute before heading out. I didn't react in any way that would reveal how keenly I was aware of her response. Though I allowed myself a smile once I'd moved past her.

She played it cool. So did I. We didn't even exchange glances for a week. And those first glances, when they came, were fleeting, as if a lingering gaze would admit too much interest.

Eventually, knowing she'd never be the first to break the silence, I spoke.

"Hello."

That was all. An opening.

"Hello, yourself."

Another week, and we were walking to school—not really together, just side by side. She told me very little about herself. I told her less about my own past.

We became friends. Not boyfriend and girlfriend, but a boy and a girl who were friends. This was better, since I would eventually betray her. No, betray is not the right word. I guess "exploit" would be better. Still, she'd feel a wound in her soul. But the wound of a friend's betrayal stings a little less than that of a beloved's deceit. Even so, I felt sad about that eventual wound. I hoped she would get over it.

Two months passed before the rumors started. First, a homeless man was found in an alley between a barber shop and a tattoo parlor. His death was attributed to blood loss. Though there was no spilled blood at the scene.

Two weeks later, a girl from our high school disappeared. The police believed she'd run away. But her friends swore she had no problems at home and no reason to leave town.

It was time.

"Let's have an adventure," I said to Lolana after school.

"Like what?" she asked.

"Let's pretend we're running away. I'll make sandwiches. We'll go off to the woods for a moonlit picnic."

She raised one eyebrow. "Are you asking me on a date?"

"No. I'm asking you on an adventure." I gave her my best innocent smile.

She touched my arm. "I'll make cookies."

I met her on the corner about an hour before sunset. I had a flashlight to help mark our way and matches to make a campfire when we got there. She had a container of fresh-baked chocolate chip cookies.

I have to say, her face looked radiant and bewitching in the light of our fire. I love the dance of light and shadows cast by flames. We sat and ate the sandwiches and still-soft cookies, and I waited for him. I knew he'd come. I just wasn't sure when or how. I hoped he wouldn't hurt her. That would make me sad.

"How lovely . . ."

The voice came from above. Good. Some of them are silent, prizing stealth. The talkers are easier to deal with. They allow themselves to get distracted by their own words. I looked up. He was perched on a tree branch overhead, his figure silhouetted against the quarter moon.

Lolana let out a gasp and clutched her chest with one hand, just below her neck. I doubt she realized the significance of this gesture.

"Huh?" I shouted, scrambling to my feet. I forced my heart to speed up, as if I'd been seized by terror. I trusted that I sounded sufficiently startled.

He dropped from the branch, landing between us as silently as a cat dropping from a couch to a carpet.

"A picnic," he said. "How lovely. May I join you?"

He bared his fangs, then laughed.

Perfect. He planned to toy with us. I wasn't surprised. Most of his kind were narcissistic fools who equated longevity with wisdom.

"No, on second thought, I don't think I'll dine *with* you," he said. "I think I'll dine *on* you. I've quite a thirst."

Lolana was trembling now. Poor girl. She looked at me as if I could rescue her.

"Who wants to be first?" he asked.

I turned and fled, stumbling and staggering away through the underbrush.

I hadn't gone far before I heard Lolana scream.

The vampire laughed. "Don't worry. I'll chase down the coward next. And he'll suffer for his lack of chivalry. But first, my dear, I need to get to know that lovely neck of yours—and the lovely blood pulsing beneath it."

He turned toward her and grabbed her shoulder. His back was to me now.

Perfect.

I closed the distance between us in an eyeblink. As I slammed against him, I reached around and put one hand beneath his chin, yanking his head back.

Lolana collapsed. She was unharmed. I could tell. But her heart had slowed. She'd fainted. Good. She didn't need to see what was about to happen.

The vampire let out a gasp of surprise and confusion. I had already arched his body backward, revealing his own neck. He struggled, but he was a mere vampire. They're strong. But just as parasites have lesser bugs to bite them, blood-sucking vampires have greater blood drinkers to feast on them.

He needed human blood once a week to survive.

I needed vampire blood once a year.

It was feeding time. I drank what I needed. Unlike a vampire, I can walk in the sun. I can eat human food, though it does not nourish me. And I can see my reflection. I saw it once when I was feeding. My eyes turned red, almost glowing. I thought it made me quite handsome and intriguing.

When I was finished feeding from the vampire, I dropped the body. In a moment, it collapsed into ashes. One strong gust of wind, and there'd be no sign left of him, and no more mysterious deaths in town. I turned my attention to Lolana. Poor girl. I'd used her as bait. But she hadn't been harmed. She wouldn't remember much of this. With luck, I'd be able to bring her to a safe location before she woke. All she'd really know is that her friend had vanished one night. As for me, I'd slip off in search of a good place to await next year's feeding.

"Sweet girl," I whispered as I stroked her hair. "You have no idea how much you helped me."

I picked her up gently to carry her back to town.

She shifted in my arms. Her eyes opened. By the time I realized the meaning of the red glow and look of long-simmering hunger, it was too late. She'd already grabbed my head and forced it back.

I struggled, but she was far stronger than I was—impossibly strong.

"I'm sorry," she said as she held me immobile. "I really liked you. But I like the blood of those who drink vampire blood even more. More than like it, I need it. But not often. Once a decade is enough."

As she clamped her mouth on my neck and feasted, I heard my grandmother reciting the rhyme about smaller bugs. I guess larger bugs have larger bugs to feast on them, too. Ad infinitum.

FROZEN IN TIME

Fudge bars!

That had to be it.

The sticky note on the fridge read: *Hope you had a good day at school. Special treat in freezer. Love, Dad.*

That was in blue pen. Below that, in pencil, was: *Just one, Alexis.*

That was from Mom, who doesn't spoil me as much as Dad does but is still pretty much a softy except when I leave a mess or forget to pick up after myself, which happens a lot because I've always got a thousand things zipping through my mind, and I get distracted pretty easily.

Please be fudge bars . . .

I opened the freezer door and felt the cold air brush my arm. When cold and warm air meet, you get convection. That's one of three forms of heat transference. There was also a visible swirl of condensation, because cooler air holds less moisture.

Oops. I realized I was standing there with the door open. I turned my attention to the contents of the freezer.

Yes!

I found myself face-to-face with an unopened box of my favorite frozen fudgy treat, Double Fudgy Choco Bars. I unzipped the cardboard strip on the end flap that stood between me and icy, sweet delight and grabbed my treat.

Bing, bong.

The doorbell rang.

Oh, fudge. I was totally looking forward to sinking into the big easy chair by the window in the living room and reading my new book as I savored my treat.

I went to the front door, stood on my tiptoes, and looked through the small glass section that was just a bit too high to be convenient. I was home alone. Mom and Dad were both at work. But I was old enough to be here by myself. And I was smart enough to know you don't just fling open the door without checking to see who's there.

"Huh?" I'm rarely startled. But Mom was on the porch. Why would she be ringing the bell? She has a key. And why did she look so young? Aging is a gradual process. I wrote a paper about it for my science class last month. Everything is controlled at the cellular level. There are these things called *telomeres* that are connected with aging.

Mom rang the bell again, pushing the button three times in rapid succession.

I opened the door.

It wasn't Mom. The woman looked like Mom did in her photos from college. Except for her eyes. Those reminded me of someone else.

She grabbed my arm and said, "I'm here from—"

Before I could pull free, she vanished. But she didn't vanish like something blinking off. She collapsed into a bright pinpoint of light and shot away from me at a forty-five-degree angle.

"I need to sit down," I said as I staggered back from the door. Great. Not only was I seeing impossible things, I was also talking to myself. I closed the door and headed for the living room. Perceptions can be altered in a variety of ways. Perhaps I'd encountered a neurotoxin of some sort. I thought back through my day to see if I'd done anything that could explain the current state of my brain.

Bing, bong.

"No . . ."

I went back to the door, peeked through the window, and saw Mom again. Still not exactly Mom, but a little bit older than she'd been a minute ago.

I pulled open the door, but stepped back so she couldn't grab my arm.

"I'm here from the future," she said. "I'm—"

Collapse, zoom, bye.

I closed the door. But I stayed where I was. Whoever I'd encountered, she seemed to have a very limited time to give me her message. I wanted to help maximize that time.

Bing, bong.

Fling.

"I'm you," she said, the instant the door opened. I guess she knew I'd already gotten the first message, about how she was from the future.

She went on. "I don't have much time." Her eyes drifted from me, and she said, "We keep extending the duration. It's all based on synchronizing subatomic particles with the right harmonics. Pretty fascinating. Anyhow, I need to tell you—"

Collapse, zoom, bye.

So that's why she looked like Mom, but had Dad's eyes. She wasn't Mom. She was me from the future.

Some kids would have a hard time believing time travel was possible. Not me. I was fascinated by it. Ever since I was little and discovered science, I've wanted to work on something spectacular and world-changing when I got out of college, like teleportation or immortality. I loved the idea that I grew up to work on time travel. And, as for proof that she was really me and not someone playing an elaborate joke, the way she—I mean I . . . or maybe we?—got distracted was exactly how I acted.

I stayed where I was, with the door open. I wanted to see her, I mean me, arrive.

As I expected, her arrival was like the zooming departure played in reverse. A bright dot shot toward me from forty-five degrees above the horizon, expanding until it became my future self on the porch.

This time, I grabbed her arm. "Get right to the message!" I said. I shivered at the possibilities a message from the future could contain. She could tell me what stock to buy, or what boy to watch out for, or even which college to go to.

But if she warned me about something, wouldn't that change the future? And then, what if, because of that change, I didn't invent time travel?

Or what if she gave me the secret to time travel! What an amazing paradox. I invent time travel, and then go back to tell myself how to invent time travel. I loved the way that idea twisted reality into a pretzel, or a Möbius strip. I imagined infinite loops of time and space.

I realized she'd been talking. And I hadn't been listening.

Collapse, zoom, bye.

I waited for the next visit. She was older than Mom this time. A lot older. It sort of creeped me out to see myself as an old lady, but it also comforted me to know that I'd live a long life.

"Alexis," she said, grabbing my arm.

"What?"

"You left your fudge bar on the counter. It's melting and dripping all over the floor. And Mom is coming home early. Hurry. Go clean up your mess."

Collapse, zoom, bye.

That was it? A lifetime spent developing and improving time travel, and "your fudge bar is melting" is the message I gave myself?

Oh, fudge. I guess I'd put it down when the bell rang.

As I headed for the kitchen to see what was left of my fudgy treat, I started thinking about giving myself a more useful message when it was my turn to come back. The fudge bar had already dripped down the side of the counter and onto the linoleum. I grabbed a paper towel.

Wait a minute . . .

The only reason I'd put the fudge bar down in the first place was because the doorbell rang. And the only reason the doorbell rang was because I'd come back to warn myself about the fudge bar. But if the future me had never come back, the present me wouldn't have needed a warning. I'd caused myself to do the very thing I'd warned myself about. And wouldn't it have been smarter to come back to a time before I took the fudge bar out of the freezer, so I could stop it from happening?

My thoughts were interrupted by the sound of the front door. This time, it was opened with a key. Mom came in and went directly to the kitchen.

I stood there, paper towel in hand. I hadn't had a chance to clean up the drips yet.

"Alexis!" Mom shouted. "Look at that mess. You are grounded."

"It's not my fault," I said.

Mom stared at me.

"Not yet, at least," I said.

Mom shook her head and walked out of the kitchen.

I realized there was no way I could explain things to her. So I got to work cleaning up my mess. This mess, at least. I'd have to wait to see how I dealt with the time-travel mess when it was my turn to go back to talk to myself. But I was sort of eager to find out.

IN WARM BLOOD

It's great being rich. I feel sorry for kids who can't have everything they want. My dad has billions. Really. Not like when someone says, "I have a billion comic books." No. It's like my tutor, Leonard, taught me. When you're just using *billions* to mean "a whole lot," that's a figurative expression. But, with my Dad, when I say *billions*, it's literal. He has at least two billion dollars. He buys me anything I want. Because, really, you can spend five or ten million without making any sort of dent in a billion.

If I wanted my own castle, I could have it. If I wanted a tank that could totally blow the castle to bits, I could have that, too. And I did.

So, when I heard about DinoShoot Adventures, and told Dad I wanted to do that, he said sure. It didn't matter that it cost twelve million dollars. For him, that was pocket change.

Dad was too busy to go with me to set things up, so he had Marsdon, our head butler, escort me to DinoShoot headquarters. Dad had already wired the money to them. They were real nice to me when I walked in. I'm used to that. Anyone who isn't nice to me is going to hear about it from Dad. One time, people were snotty to me in a clothing store, so Dad bought the store and fired all the employees. I stood by the door and watched as they left. Two of the women were crying. I enjoyed seeing them get the treatment they deserved.

When we got to DinoShoot, a receptionist sent us right in to the main office. "Welcome, Kenneth," a man in a nicely tailored suit and light-blue silk shirt said. "I'm Mr. Fuller. I'll be helping you select the subject of your Primordial Harvesting Experience."

Primordial Harvesting Experience? That didn't sound like fun. "I'm here to blow away a dinosaur," I said. I held up my hands like I was clutching a rifle, and I fired off a shot. "Bang!"

"Of course," he said. "That's exactly the experience we offer. You will be able to harvest—I mean, blow away—the dinosaur of your choice. Do you have a species in mind, or would you like to browse the offerings?" He pointed to a touch screen that covered most of the wall behind his desk. It was filled with photographs of dinosaurs.

But I'd already given my choice a lot of thought. The tyrannosaurus is the best-known carnivore, except maybe for the velociraptors from *Jurassic Park*. And the brontosaurus, or apatosaurus, is the biggest commonly known dinosaur. But hunting a huge herbivore would be like going after an enormous cow. It wouldn't be the kind of thrill I needed. I wanted to combine large and dangerous, and take on the biggest carnivore. That would give me a trophy my friends would envy.

"Spinosaurus," I said. The name wasn't as cool as *Giganotosaurus*, but the spinosaurus was bigger, and its head would look awesome in my game room.

"Very good." Mr. Fuller smiled and nodded, like the waiters do at the fancy restaurants Dad takes me to when he's celebrating a business victory. "Let's get you trained and outfitted."

"Trained?" I asked.

"You will be using an extremely high-powered weapon," he said. "It's been engineered to reduce recoil as much as possible, but it's still best to get the feel of it before starting your adventure."

"I'm an expert," I said. One of Dad's businesses sells weapons. He's let me try out most of them. I could handle whatever they gave me. I've even fired a rocket launcher.

"Very well." Mr. Fuller pressed a button on his desk. A guy dressed in safari clothes came in through a side door. He looked tough enough to fight a rhino bare-handed.

Mr. Fuller introduced us. "This is Darrin Claymore. He's our top guide. We reserve him for only our most important and valued clients. He'll take good care of you."

Darrin held out his hand. We shook. His grip was so solid, I felt like I'd wedged my hand between two rocks. "It will be the experience of a lifetime, lad," he said.

I normally don't like being called things like *lad* or *son*. But the way Darrin said it, the word sounded right.

I followed him to a private room that contained an assortment of outfits for me to choose from. "The environment will be wet and hot," Darrin said. "The Cretaceous is pretty much a swampfest."

"Mosquitos?" I asked.

"As big as your head." He tapped a holster at his belt. "I'll handle them."

I selected lightweight but strong clothing that would protect me from scratches and bites, but not get too hot. After that, Darrin took me to the armory.

"This is the only one that will stop the biggest brutes," he said, handing me a rifle with a muzzle that was at least three inches wide. I couldn't even guess the caliber, but it had to be enormous. I could see a variety of mechanisms, including springs and counterweights, along the barrel, and a small canister of compressed CO_2 right in front of the trigger. I guess that was the stuff that suppressed the recoil.

Darrin showed me where the safety was and how to load a round into the chamber. Then he picked up a bandoleer with extra ammo. Each bullet was about the size of a bowling pin.

"Are you sure you don't want to try it out on the range?" he asked. "The kick is pretty impressive."

"I know what I'm doing," I said.

"Good enough, lad. I can see you're a man of action. So am I. Let's do it."

I followed him down the hall to the other end of the building. The huge room we entered was filled with the sort of electronic equipment you'd see for controlling a space launch.

"This way." Darrin climbed the three steps that led to a platform in the middle of the room. There were two padded chairs on it.

"Take a seat. You'll feel a bit dizzy for a moment," he said.

I sat. So did Darrin.

The room grew brighter. I felt as if I were sliding headfirst down a steep hill. Everything around me stretched out, like the universe was made of taffy. Then it all shot back into place.

I wasn't in the room anymore. The cool air of the lab had been replaced with steam. I was surrounded by giant plants in a damp, hot forest. I blinked and tried to adjust to the sudden change. Even though the air was steamy, the sunlight was bright enough to make me squint at first.

Darrin held up a device with a screen in front and a large antenna on top. "Tracker," he said. "It picks up all life forms larger than two tons."

That would include the spinosaurus. It weighed twenty tons. I could see various blips on the screen. I pointed at the biggest dot. "Is that one?"

Darrin shook his head. "Too small. But we're in the right region. Come on—let's take a hike."

I followed him, sticking to the path he wove through the towering plants. Fairly soon, we saw a large herbivore grazing in a clearing. "Want something easy?" Darrin asked. "You can bag this monster and be home in time for lunch."

"No thanks."

We pushed on. It was hard moving through the jungle, but I was in great shape. Last year, Dad bought me a membership in the best gym in town, and my trainer made sure I got a good workout. After about two hours, Darrin stopped in his tracks and tapped the screen.

"Thar she blows," he said.

"Huh?" I had no idea what he was talking about.

"I found one. Big one. Biggest I've ever seen. What a trophy this is going to be, lad. We'll both be bragging about this beauty for years. Come on, it's just across that ridge."

I could feel my blood pumping through my veins in anticipation of the kill as I followed Darrin up a steep slope. We had to work our way around several gaping pits and past two thick stands of dense plant growth.

When we crested the ridge, I gasped. The spinosaurus was even larger than I could have imagined. It was like a bulldozer had grown spines and come to life. Not like a regular earth mover you'd see on a construction site, but one of the gigantic ones you see at the bottom of mines and quarries.

"Wow . . ." I let the word drift from my mouth.

"Yeah, wow," Darrin said. "What a beauty. Ready to kill it?"

A spark of doubt crossed my mind as I heard his bluntly phrased words, but it was drowned by the idea of blowing the spinosaurus away with one perfectly placed shot. "Yeah. I'm ready." I raised the rifle.

"Hold on," Darrin said, putting a hand on my arm. "It's too far away. Besides—it's more fun to shoot them when they're charging straight at you. There's no feeling like it."

"How do we get it to charge?" I asked.

"*We* don't. *I* do," he said. "That's why they pay me such a generous salary. Wait here."

He headed down the ridge until he was about fifty yards from the dinosaur. Then he shouted and waved his hands. I wondered whether something so big would even notice something so relatively small. But I guess you don't get to be that big a carnivore without paying attention to every opportunity for a meal.

The spinosaurus charged toward Darrin, who ran toward me. The earth vibrated beneath my feet like a massive coal train was passing by. I raised the rifle, sighted on the dinosaur through the scope, and waited for the ping that would tell me my target was within range. The stock and barrel were heavy, but I managed to keep them level.

The rifle *pinged.*

I fired at the dinosaur's chest.

"Ahhhh!" The scream shot from me as I got slammed in my own chest with the recoil.

The kick knocked me right off my feet and sent me tumbling backward. The spinosaurus was still charging. I fell hard and kept rolling. I caught a blurry view of Darrin, halfway down the hill, leaping to the side and whipping around his own rifle as the spinosaurus thundered past him.

I felt the hill drop out from under me. I'd rolled into one of the pits. I slammed down to the bottom. Overhead, the sun was blotted out as the spinosaurus reached the edge of the pit. It stood there, looking down at me like I was lunch. From this angle, it seemed impossibly tall. Then, the head moved lower and the jaws opened.

The pit was narrow at the bottom. Probably too narrow for the head to fit. But I wasn't taking any chances. Ignoring the pain of the recoil, I fired three more shots, aiming below the head, where the heart had to be, emptying the chamber.

I could tell from its eyes that I had killed it. But it was too stupid to know it was dead yet. In a moment, the brain and body would agree that life had come to an end, and I'd have my trophy.

"Got you!" I shouted. I'd never felt my heart beating with such stunning force. Darrin was right. There was no thrill like shooting a charging beast. I loaded another round into the chamber and shot it again, just for fun. I wanted to get my money's worth. Okay—Dad's money. But this was my adventure. This was my greatest moment.

The spinosaurus fell forward. It dropped right over the opening of the pit, sealing me in darkness.

My heart and body leaped from excitement to panic. I was trapped! For a moment, I lost control of my breathing. Then I reminded myself that Darrin would dig me out. Worst case, he'd go back for heavy equipment. They needed it to bring home the dinosaur trophy, anyhow. One way or another, all I had to do was wait to be rescued. The spinosaurus was no longer a threat. The pit was too narrow for it to fall in and crush me.

"Sit tight," I said out loud. "You just blew away a dinosaur."

To prove I was still in control, I fired another shot straight up at it.

Something splashed on my head.

I felt a warm, sticky liquid on my face. More of it flooded down around me.

Dinosaur blood.

It was filling the pit.

I dropped the rifle and scrambled for the side of the pit. It was slick with blood. I tried to climb, but I fell back.

The blood rose to my knees, then to my waist. I listened for any sound of rescue, but all I heard was a gushing torrent, like someone emptying a large bucket. An endless bucket.

Soon, the pool of blood reached my chest. I floated up until I bumped against the body of the dinosaur.

Too soon, the blood reached my neck, and then my chin.

I'd killed a dinosaur.

And now, it was killing me.

THE DUGGLY UCKLING

There once was a duck who sat on a nest near the edge of a small pond, tending her eggs and dreaming of the days when the hatchlings would follow her as she swam across the calm surface of the water. Finally, after what seemed like forever, one of the eggs started to wiggle and shake.

"It's time," she quacked.

One by one, the eggs hatched, revealing little fluff balls of cuteness.

"Aren't they lovely?" she asked.

"Indeed they are," said a passing robin.

Soon, there were six little ducklings drying their feathers in the afternoon sunlight. But a seventh egg didn't hatch. The mother watched it, fearing it might never open. The thought cast a shadow on this joyful day.

But, just after the sun set and darkness gripped the pond, the seventh egg shook as the shell was pecked at from within. Eventually, the seventh duckling emerged.

Even in the dim light of the moon, the duck and the other

ducklings could see the new hatchling well enough to know that this one was different.

"Not pretty," the mother said.

"Worse than that," said duckling number one. "Look at those ugly feathers."

"Too ugly to be a duckling," said number two. "And what a strange shade of yellow."

"Right!" said number three. "That's not a duckling. It's an uckling."

"A duggly uckling," said number four. "With a big, fat bill."

Number five and number six were too busy gagging to add their comments.

As for the duggly uckling, she stood there, sad and lonely, wondering why her welcome into the world had been so harsh and cruel. In the morning, she waddled away.

The next day, as the uckling searched for somewhere to call home, she met a rabbit.

"What are you?" the rabbit asked.

"A duckling," the uckling said.

"Too ugly," the rabbit said.

The uckling didn't answer. But her heart grew heavier.

Next, she met a frog, who said, "You're so ugly, you make me want to croak."

That was followed by a deer, a swallow, a turtle, a turkey, and a dozen other animals, all of whom agreed that the uckling was ugly.

The uckling traveled farther and farther from the pond, in search of someone who would appreciate her. Finally, after more than a year had passed, and the uckling had grown much bigger, she met a warthog.

"I know," the uckling said. "I'm ugly."

"Not at all," the warthog said. "I know all about ugly, and you don't qualify."

"But ducklings don't look like me," she said. "And all the animals say I'm ugly."

"Of course ducklings don't look like you," the warthog said. "You're not a duckling. You're a dragon."

"Dragon?" the uckling asked.

"Absolutely. A beautiful, yellow-green dragon, with shiny scales and a marvelous snout."

"Are you sure?" the uckling asked.

"Try breathing fire," the warthog said. "Wait! Turn your head first."

The uckling turned her head and blew a puff of fire. "I didn't know I could do that," she said.

"Now try flying," the warthog said.

The uckling sprouted her amazing wings and gave a flap. She rose into the air. Then she flew off.

"Where are you going?" the warthog asked. "I like you. You can stay here."

But the uckling had flown out of sight.

Happily, she returned a while later, clutching something in her claws.

"What's that?" the warthog asked.

"A present," the uckling said. "I hope you like crispy roast duck."

"Love it," the warthog said.

And so the ugly warthog and the beautiful dragon had their first of many wonderful meals together. And they lived happily, and deliciously, ever after.

SPELL BINDING

I love old books. My friends think I'm weird. They love clothing, jewelry, and the latest gadget. But books are my trea-
sures. That's why I walk all over town every year during the
community-wide garage sale. I didn't have much luck finding
anything good this year until I was all the way on the other
side of town. That's when I saw a stack of books on the corner
of one of the half-dozen tables in the driveway of an old house
on Sycamore Street. I picked up the top book from the stack
and ran my fingers over its flaking leather cover.

"Cool," I said. The book looked older than anything I owned.
Even before I opened it, I could tell the pages had turned yellow
and crumbly. On the first page, hand-printed in pen in an old-
fashioned style, far neater than the way we write in school—
except for that annoying Martha Senglemonger, who thinks
she's all so perfect and better than anyone—were the words:

Major Arcana
Uncovered by Simon Albergensis
Anno Domini 1793

38

Wow. That was old. I looked across the table, where a man was explaining to a woman why he couldn't sell a $50 set of wrenches to her for three dollars.

I looked at the book again. There was a stickie in front with $200 written on it. No way. No way at all, never ever. That was more than I'd spend on a whole shelf full of books.

But I had to have it.

I checked out the other books on the table. There was one that looked a lot like the book I wanted, except that the leather felt fake. I flipped past the title page to find the copyright date. The book was just ten years old. I turned back to the cover. The price was $5.

I watched the man. He was watching the lady who'd wanted the wrenches as she walked away empty-handed. A man picked up a stack of magazines and said, "Two dollars, right?"

"Right," the guy behind the table said.

"Great." The man tossed two dollars into a cash box and left with his purchase.

It's just wrong for anyone to ask so much for a book, I thought. He wasn't being fair, but I could fix that. As he turned his attention to a woman whose twin toddlers were about to grab a stack of fragile drinking glasses, I swapped the two stickies. Then, staying where I was, I held up the book and said, "Hey, Mister. Would you take four?"

Barely glancing my way, he said, "Five, kid. Firm. Take it or leave it. I'm sick of haggling with cheapskates."

"Oh, all right. You win." I tossed a five-dollar bill in the cigar box and walked off with the book, forcing myself not to run until I reached the corner.

Score!

I waited until I got home to take a close look at my new

treasure. I knew the pages would be fragile, and I didn't want to risk turning them while I was I walking. As soon as I got to my room, I opened the cover and turned past the title page. The next page just read: *One must move slowly through the arcane arts. Each discovery is a key to the next.*

On the next page, there was a spell. It was a little hard to read everything. The letters were written in a fancy style with lots of curls and swirls, and some words were spelled in weird ways. But the spell was simple. *Keep Milk from Spoiling.*

That didn't interest me. We have a fridge. And if the milk spoiled, there was a corner store two blocks away that was open 24/7. I turned the page. Or tried to. It was stuck. I tried to lift it at the top and at the bottom. I even tried slipping a fingernail under a corner. No luck. It was as if the rest of the book were a solid block.

"Stupid book," I said. I tossed it into my closet.

But later that day, I got curious, and went online to see if there was any information about this Simon Albergensis. It turned out he'd been sort of famous, way back in the 1700s. He'd lived in London, and claimed to be a sorcerer. There were rumors that he had created a spell for eternal life. He was murdered by his great rival, Roderick Magnatesta, just before his ninety-seventh birthday. Magnatesta was caught right after the murder, as he was searching through his victim's house. He was executed for his crime. One article I found ended with: *Had he not been murdered, Simon Albergensis might have lived forever.*

"Lived forever . . ." I said out loud. I retrieved the book from my closet and studied the edges of the pages. Maybe that immortality spell was trapped in there. It might be possible to separate the pages. But there was no point in bothering with that unless I could prove that his spells worked. And that would be easy enough to do. I could try the milk spell.

I grabbed two glasses from the kitchen and put some milk in each. They'd taught us in science class how an experiment needs a control sample to compare against the sample being tested. After I poured the milk, I gathered the material for the spell. I found every ingredient I needed, except for a sliver of willow bark, right in my kitchen. And the bark was easy to find right down the street from me. I mixed a variety of herbs in a bowl, along with a splash of vinegar and the piece of bark. I chanted the words that were listed, soaked a clean piece of knitted wool in the mixture—good thing I have lots of scarves—and tied the cloth around one of the glasses.

This will never work, I thought as I carried the two glasses up to our attic, which got very warm this time of year. I left the glasses there, figuring that the milk would definitely be sour by the next morning.

When I woke, I went right up to check the milk. As I lifted the trap door to the attic, a rotten odor hit my nose. Yeesh. The milk had definitely gone sour. I picked up the glass without the wool. It smelled awful. I didn't need to taste it to know it had spoiled. I took the glass downstairs and poured the milk out in the sink, then rinsed everything with some water.

I went back to the attic. The smell lingered, but it wasn't as strong. I picked up the other glass and gave it a careful sniff.

It smelled like fresh milk. I took a tiny sip, bracing myself for an unpleasant experience.

It seemed fine.

I took a bigger sip.

The milk was warm, but it tasted as fresh as ever.

The spell worked!

I drank the rest of the milk, then ran to my room to grab the book.

As I opened it to the milk spell, the page lifted slightly. It had become unstuck.

A shiver ran through my body, as if I'd chugged a large glass of ice-cold milk. I turned to the new page and discovered a spell for making it rain. How could I resist? It was a sunny day, without a cloud in the sky. I had to go into the woods behind the school to find one of the plants I needed, and I gagged a little when I scooped up the earthworm I'd uncovered, as instructed, from a hole dug from shaded ground near an iron fence. But early that afternoon, I danced in the rain, laughing like I owned the world and everything in it. Which might not have been far from the truth, depending on what spells lay ahead.

I dried my hands before opening the book. The page with the rain spell was loose. I turned it.

As I read over the spell for banishing all insects from an area of three hectares—whatever that meant—I wondered how far away the immortality spell was. The book wasn't very thick. Maybe there were seventy or eighty pages. I was getting impatient with unspoiled milk and rain-on-demand. Still, I did the insect spell. It was easy enough. But I didn't bother trying to check to see if it worked.

The next spell was for a way to treat a purple shirt so it would resist all flames. I made the shirt, which had to be worn during the final stage of the spell, but didn't test it out with fire. I was pretty sure all the spells worked, but I had no desire to find myself in a burning shirt. Besides, I was eager to get to the next spell.

I turned the page and froze. I stared down, surprised by the unexpected difference. All the other pages had been white, with words written in dark-brown ink. This page was black, inscribed with silver ink.

The spell was, "To slay your mortal enemy."

That was a problem. I didn't have a mortal enemy. I wasn't going to slay anyone. Though there were two or three kids in the neighborhood I wouldn't mind hurting a bit.

Just the idea of murder made me start to sweat. I opened the window in my bedroom, then went back to the book.

I can't slay someone.

Still, unless I cast the spell, I'd never be able to turn the page. Which meant I'd never reach the spell that would make me live forever. And I needed to reach that spell. Maybe there was some sort of balance to the magic. To live forever, you first had to take another life. I thought about how amazing it would be to live through a thousand years of history. I couldn't even imagine what new technologies there'd be. Maybe I could even walk on Mars, or visit a city built beneath the ocean. I needed to live forever. I deserved it. It was my right!

There had to be someone I could cast the death spell on. I smiled as a handful of candidates came to mind. I realized I felt totally calm as I narrowed the list down. That's when I knew I could really do it.

I read the spell. In old language, with lots of "haths" and "thines," it said, "Have your victim drink bespelled milk. Have your victim dance in bespelled rain."

My hands clutched the book tighter.

"Have your victim stand in bespelled land, free of insects. Have your victim wear a purple shirt, bespelled to ward off fire."

I dropped the book, but it remained open, and my eyes couldn't avoid the final line.

"Have your victim cast stolen spells."

As if a hot wind had blown through the room, the page turned on its own, revealing a message for someone who had perished centuries ago.

"Thus I exact my vengeance on you, Roderick Magnatesta, for I knew you would slay me and steal my work. I laid this trap because the greedy are easy to ensnare, and you are the greediest of all. Perish, fool. Vengeance is mine, for I know your death will not come until you've suffered great pain."

"No!" I screamed. "I'm not him!"

The shirt grew hotter. And tighter. I ripped at it, but it wouldn't tear.

"No!" I screamed again, as the heat became unbearable. On the table, the page turned again. It was blank. This was the last spell. There was no everlasting life.

For me, there was only the opposite.

STRIKEOUT OF THE BLEACHER WEENIES

I **used to love** baseball. I played every summer in my old town. When I moved to Shrepsburg, I was happy to see the town had a league. And Mom was happy I signed up. She can't come to the games very often because she works two jobs, but she's glad I have something to do. I went to the tryouts and got picked by the Phantoms.

The league was also a good way to make friends. I got to know Doug, Willy, Adam, and most of the other guys pretty well, but I guess my closest friend by the end of the season was Gordy. That's weird, since he's a total nerd, and I'm not. I met him before our first practice, when Mom dropped me off at the field. Everyone else was tossing balls around. Gordy was sitting on the first row of the bleachers with his face buried in a book.

"*String Theory and the Superluminal Neutrino,*" I said, reading the title aloud. I stumbled a bit on *superluminal.*

He looked up and smiled. "It could be the key to teleportation, though string theory is being challenged. Still, an intriguing read."

"Right." I started to turn away.

"Gordy," he said, holding out his hand. "You're new."

"Lance," I said. "I am." We shook. His grip was not that of a nerd. Later, I found out he liked to go rock climbing.

The coach, Mr. Parker, called us together and gave us a quick talk. "We're here to play baseball," he said. "We're here to do our best. To learn. To have fun. And to win."

I noticed he put winning last in his list, and he didn't shout the word, like my last coach did.

I fit right in with the team, even though I was the new kid. Baseball is a universal language. I got to play third base because I have a good arm and fast reflexes. I can snag a sizzling grounder that's hopping like a runaway bottle rocket, and make the throw to first fast enough to beat most runners.

Opening day, we played the Cruisers. Since all the teams in the league are from town, we take turns being "home" and "visitor." The bleacher along the first base line was considered the home-team side, and the one along third was for the away team. There was no real rule or sign. It was just one of those things everyone in town knows. Today, we were the visitors.

"Wow, a lot of people came," I said when we took our seats in the dugout, which was actually just a bench. Both bleachers were filled. Some people brought lawn chairs, others stood near the fence that ran between the bleachers and the base lines. I saw three people on our side with "Go Phantoms!" signs. The other side had at least a dozen signs.

"The league is a big thing around here," Gordy said. I noticed he was now reading *Parallel Universes and the Space-Time Continuum*.

"My parents and both my uncles came," Adam said.

"My dad and my grandmom are here," Willy said.

"My mom's here," I said. I glanced over my shoulder at her. She'd managed to get some time off, but she'd have to leave before the game ended. Still, it was great she'd come.

As the Crusiers took the field, I heard a shriek from the home-team bleachers. A woman holding a sign that read KILL 'EM, CRUISERS!!!!! (yeah, that's how she spelled it) leaped out of her seat and ran over to the Crusiers' coach, screaming, "Left field?! No way! Not my Howie!"

"Here we go," Gordy said.

"That was quick," Doug said.

Nobody on our team seemed at all surprised by the outburst.

From what I could tell, the woman was furious that her son had been placed in left field instead of at first base where she felt he belonged.

The coach talked to her for a moment. She screamed some more, then stormed over to her son and dragged him away.

"Good grief," I said. "What's her problem? I like the outfield." That was true. You might not get as much action, but you get a chance to save the day with a spectacular catch, and you get to make some heroic throws.

"She's a Bleacher Weenie," Gordy said.

That earned him a puzzled stare from me.

"You'll see," he said.

And I saw. During the six innings of our game, two Crusiers dads and a mom exploded over things that shouldn't have bothered anyone, one couple got thrown off the field after going ballistic about a close call, and a grandmother holding a Pomeranian staged a brief sit-down protest right in front of the mound after the Crusiers' coach changed pitchers.

"Is it always like this?" I asked Gordy as we lined up at the end of the game to let the losing team congratulate us, and for us to tell them "good try." Not that there was much sincerity on either side.

"It's usually worse," he said.

That was not good news. Something else hit me as we were leaving the field. "The Bleacher Weenies were all on the other side," I said. I realized nobody who was rooting for the Phantoms had acted out.

"Mr. Parker picks his team based on the parents," Gordy said.

"That's pretty smart," I said. "I'm glad he took a chance with me."

The next game, the Bleacher Weenies rooting for the other team were even worse. Every single close call turned into a shouting match. "I hope this is as bad as it gets," I said after we'd squeaked through a narrow one-to-nothing win.

"Just wait," Adam said.

"Yeah, we're playing the Aztecs next," Willy said.

"How could it be worse?" I asked.

"They have Nolan Gruber and Horse-head Shaw," Gordy said. "Their parents are the worst."

"And they've never been on the same team before," Adam said.

"They also have both Carson twins and Ralphie Baltzinger," Doug said. "Those kids' parents are almost as bad as Mr. Gruber."

"This could get epic," Gordy said. "We might see Bleacher Weenies achieve critical mass." He slapped his book, *Sociological Aspects of Recreation and Worship in Pre-Columbian Mesoamerican Cultures*, for emphasis.

Part of me was dreading the next game. All the yelling and

bad sportsmanship took away from our fun. And, as bad as it was to see an adult yell and scream at a coach or umpire, it was really awful to see one yell at a kid. Some of the Bleacher Weenies not only had no problem screaming at their own offspring in public but they also didn't seem to realize how bad it was to scream at someone else's kid.

So, yeah, there was dread. But there was also a small part of me that enjoyed seeing a grown-up make a fool of himself. Or herself. I'm not proud of that. But I'm human.

Nolan Gruber was the Aztecs' pitcher. Horse-head Shaw was the catcher. His nickname was, if anything, an understatement.

Before the game, I studied the people in the bleachers, trying to pick out Nolan's and Horse-head's fathers. I was pretty sure they were the guys with the biggest, rudest signs, sitting side by side at the top of the bleachers. One had a Yankees shirt on. The other wore a Mets shirt.

"Wait," I said to Doug when we took our seats on the bench. Something had been tickling my mind after seeing all the Aztecs signs and shirts. "I thought we weren't supposed to have teams named after groups of people."

"Their coach is a jerk," Doug said, motioning toward the Aztecs' bench with his head. "But he donates a lot of money to the league. He fought for the name, and they crumpled."

This is definitely going to be interesting, I thought when the umpire yelled, "Play ball!"

That was also an understatement.

Here's one more understatement: Nolan wasn't having a good first inning. He kept missing the strike zone, and walked enough of us that we were up three to nothing before even getting an out.

Then, the two guys from the top of the Aztecs' bleachers

slinked over behind the backstop. On Nolan's first pitch to Adam, the guy in the Yankees shirt yelled "Good one!" even though it was clearly a ball. The umpire didn't fall for it that time. Or the next, when the Mets guy yelled, "Nice pitch! Right over the plate!" By then, three other Aztecs parents had joined the party. The crowd must have swayed the ump, or distracted him, because he called the third and fourth pitches strikes, even though they were wide.

"That's cheating," Gordy said. "Umps try to be neutral, but the influence of the mob is a factor." He smacked the book sitting next to him: *Extraordinary Popular Delusions and the Madness of Crowds.*

So the count was two and two, and Adam was rattled. He swung at the next pitch, even though it was almost low enough to bounce off the plate.

Strike three.

I caught coach Parker's eye. He shrugged. "Nothing I can do," he said.

As well-behaved as the parents normally were on our side, they were quickly dragged down to the level of the Bleacher Weenies. By the third inning, half the parents on each side were crowded behind the backstop. One group was screaming "Good pitch!" while the other yelled stuff like, "Good eye, batter!" or "That's a ball!"

At the bottom of the last inning, we still had only three runs, while the Aztecs had scored five.

"This will not end well," Gordy said as he walked up to the plate.

He was more right than he realized. Nolan was getting so rattled, he clipped Gordy on the shoulder with a pitch. Gordy was hurt, but he shook it off and took first. Willy hit a line drive that got him safely on base. I was up next. I tried to shut out all the shouting. I also tried to stay alert for wild pitches.

The first pitch was low and outside, but not super low and not super outside. I like them that way. And I liked the idea of putting an end to the game before one of the parents took a swing at another and started a riot.

I clocked the ball, smacking it right over the fence.

I might have failed to mention that I'm a pretty good hitter. That, too, is an understatement. As I dropped my bat, I noticed Nolan's father was glaring at me like he wanted to knock me over the outfield fence. I gave him a shrug and a smile, then rounded the bases.

"I love shallow parabolic arcs," Gordy said as he took his turn slapping my raised hand after I'd crossed home plate.

That might have been nerd-speak, but I knew enough math to nod and smile.

So we won. But nobody was happy about the way the Bleacher Weenies had acted. The league had an emergency meeting the next evening and passed a rule banning parents from standing behind the backstop.

The next time we played the Aztecs, Nolan's father brought an air horn, and Horse-head's father brought a whistle. They blasted their noisemakers whenever anyone on our side was about to swing at a crucial pitch.

That led to another emergency meeting. Air horns and whistles were banned. The league was smart enough to make the ban broad enough to cover "any noisemaking or distracting device."

The problem is, it's a small league, so we play each team four or five times. The next time we faced the Aztecs, I made a grab for a sizzler Nolan hit. I didn't snag it, but I managed to knock it down, then scoop it up and burn one to first. The throw just beat the runner.

The umpire called him out. It was the correct call.

Nolan's father exploded from the bleachers and ran right onto the field. He started screaming at the umpire. That got him ejected from the field. But on his way out, he walked past third base. He moved so close to me, I could feel the heat from his red face. He pointed a shaking finger at me and yelled, "You'll get yours!"

The fourth time we played the Aztecs, Nolan hit a double. As he was taking his lead off second, his father yelled something to him. It sounded like, "Here's your chance." Nolan nodded, and then he grinned in my direction. I had the feeling he was going to try to take me out when he ran to third. We were the only team that had beaten them so far this year, and I guess I got a lot of the credit, or blame, for that. Which made me a target.

The next batter hit one down the first-base line. Adam scooped it up, tagged first, then threw to me at third. Nolan was charging at me like he had no plans to slide or slow down. I stood my ground.

It was a good throw, just slightly wide. I had to lean to snag it, but I made a tag. Nolan slammed into me. I thought I was braced, but I went flying.

I hit the ground hard.

Really hard.

The ground shouldn't have been this hard.

I got to my feet, pushing off the hard stones.

I felt a warm breeze blow across my chest. I checked to see if I'd ripped my shirt. I hadn't ripped it. I'd lost it. My gut clenched as I realized I wasn't wearing much of anything. I was in elbow pads, knee pads, and some sort of very short shorts.

So was everyone else. My whole team. Everyone wore about as little as I did. Each of us had a slash of red paint across our chest. We were on a field in a stone stadium. The seats were filled with people who were cheering and shouting.

A large ball, twice the size of a soccer ball, whizzed past me. "Got it," someone shouted.

It was Mr. Gruber, Nolan's dad. He smacked the ball in the other direction with his head.

Mr. Gruber?

They were all there. All the worst of the Bleacher Weenies— mostly parents from the Aztecs' side, but also some bad sports from other teams. They had blue slashes on their chests. We were playing some sort of game against them.

If anyone had a clue why we were here, it would be Gordy. I looked around for him. He spotted me at the same time.

"What's going on?" I called as I jogged toward him.

Before Gordy could answer, Mr. Gruber knocked him off his feet.

Whatever we were playing, that had to be some kind of foul. I didn't see any referee. Mr. Gruber kept running. He hit the ball with his elbow. It almost went into a hole in a stone disk at one side of the court. The crowd went wild.

"I don't like this," I said when I reached Gordy.

"It's definitely not a good situation," he said.

Someone shouted my name. I turned just in time to see Doug give the ball a solid whack with his knee, sending it back down the field toward me. Now that I knew what I had to do, it was easy. I deflected the ball with my shoulder, sending it to

Alex, who was near the goal. He tried to put it in. But the hole in the stone was really small.

Things got rough. The Bleacher Weenies were bigger and stronger, but we were in a lot better shape, we knew how to play sports, and we understood the value of teamwork.

Still, possession and momentum went back and forth, like a volleyball game where the serving side keeps losing the ball.

I noticed Gordy was standing off to the side, staring at the crowd.

I ran over to him. "You okay?"

"That's it!" he said. "Amazing!"

"What?" I asked.

He grabbed my arm. "This has to be your doing!"

"How do you know that?" I asked.

"Because it isn't accurate. These aren't Aztecs. I know that, but you probably don't. You sucked us into the wrong version of reality, based on your hazy beliefs and memories. I need to think. I know who they are. I'm just feeling disoriented. . . ."

Across the field, the Bleacher Weenies almost scored. "We can talk about this later," I said. I had a feeling we needed to win. The next time I got an opening, I took the ball all the way to the ring. Just when I was about to score, I got tackled from behind.

I sprang back up, ready to shout at Mr. Gruber. But it wasn't him. It was Gordy.

"What was that for?" I asked. "We were about to win. It would be awesome to beat the Bleacher Weenies."

"Mayans!" he said. "That's who they are. Didn't you learn about them in school?"

I had no idea what he was talking about.

"The ancient Mayans played this game," he said. "Guess how they celebrated a victory."

"How?" I asked. I vaguely remembered I was always mixing up the Incas, Mayans, and Aztecs.

"They sacrificed the winners," he said.

Just as he said that, I saw Mr. Gruber knock down two of our players and score a goal.

"Or maybe it was the losers . . ." Gordy said. "There's some debate among the experts."

The crowd swarmed the field. Gordy's eyes got wider. "They're going to cut our heads off! That's how they did it back then."

We got separated by the mob. They lifted us red slashers onto their shoulders. They dragged the blue slashers to slabs of rocks right next to the field.

"I guess it is the winners," Gordy shouted.

Men were standing by each of the Bleacher Weenies, holding knives.

One of them raised his knife right above Mr. Gruber's heart. It looked like the decapitation part wasn't right, either. Not that it made all that much difference in the long run.

"No!" I shouted. He might be a Bleacher Weenie and a terrible person, but he didn't deserve to have his heart cut out. A kidney, maybe. But not a heart.

I dived off the shoulders I was perched on, and hit the ground hard, hoping I could save Mr. Gruber.

Someone scrambled over me, trying to get back in contact with third base. I lay where I'd tumbled to a stop, several feet into foul territory but no longer several thousand years from where I belonged.

"Out!" the umpire shouted at Nolan.

I got up from the ground, dizzy. My teammates were clustered around me.

"You okay?" Gordy asked.

"Yeah." I looked down at my shirt. It was ripped at the neck. The tear ran through the word *Phantoms*. I was back where I was supposed to be, standing on a baseball field with metal bleachers, not stone steps flanked by statues and sacrificial altars. Maybe I had a concussion.

"Did we? . . . Were we? . . ." I stared at Gordy. If it had been something I dreamed while I was knocked out, he wouldn't know what I was talking about.

"Yeah," Gordy said. "Mayans." He pointed at my chest.

I looked down, again. There was a faint slash of red on my chest. It had really happened.

Nolan was screaming at the ump about the call. "He blocked the base! That's interference! I'm not out!"

I knew someone else who would also start screaming—if he was still alive.

I turned my attention to the bleachers. All the parents we'd played against were back in their seats. They seemed dazed. Several of them were probing their chests, as if feeling for wounds. Nolan's father, his face red with rage, opened his mouth to yell at the ump. But then his face got pale, as if he suddenly remembered something very disturbing. His eyes grew wide, as if he were staring at a knife plunging toward him. Or staring at the memory of a knife. He closed his mouth. And he sunk down in his seat. His sign dropped from his hands and fluttered to the ground.

"I thought he was going to yell," Gordy said.

"I don't think he has the heart for it anymore," I said. As my words echoed in my ears, I realized how perfect they were.

I guess Gordy realized the same thing. "Too true," he said. "Hey, you know how this play should be recorded in the score book?" he asked.

"How?"

"A sacrifice," he said.

We laughed. And then we got back into the game and played our hearts out.

That's when I knew I loved baseball again.

CAMPING OUT

For a moment, right after she woke, Leandra had no idea where she was, why her bed felt so firm, why her blanket was wrapped so snugly around her body, or why the curtains on her bedroom window weren't tinted with a glow from the porch light on the house across the street. Her friend Rachel's parents never remembered to turn off that light. Leandra didn't mind. The glow provided just enough illumination for her to find her way to the hall if she needed to get a drink of water or use the bathroom in the middle of the night.

As she started to sit up, and felt resistance, Leandra realized the simple explanation for all of her observations—she was camping. Her family and three other families had gone to Cambric Mountain Scenic Campground for a weekend trip. She, Rachel, and two other friends were sharing a tent. Her older brother was in the next tent, with some of his friends. And her parents were in the tent next to that. Her sleeping bag, which she had mistaken for her covers in the brief confusion of her transition to wakefulness, was on top of a small cot.

I wonder what time it is. Leandra reached for her flashlight.

She wanted to use the light to check her watch. Then, she remembered that her watch was at home, along with her phone, her tablet, and all her essential electronic entertainment.

We're going back to nature, her dad had said.

No modern conveniences, her mom said.

The flashlight was the one exception. Leandra was surprised her parents hadn't insisted on candles or torches. But light of some sort was necessary. The campground was so far from any towns, or even any houses, that there was no light at night other than the stars, the moon, and the campfire.

Clouds had masked the starlight. The campfire had been extinguished at bedtime. A flashlight was essential for safely finding the latrines, which were on a twisting path far enough downhill from the tents that they'd be difficult to locate in the dark.

Since she had no watch to check, there was no point in turning on the flashlight now. Besides, she'd probably wake Rachel, who was a light sleeper.

Not like Bethany, Leandra thought. Bethany snored, and refused to believe it when Leandra and Rachel told her, so they finally recorded her during their last sleepover and played the proof for her the next morning.

She's not snoring now.

Leandra slowed her own breath and listened. Bethany was silent. So was the fourth tent-mate, Treena. Even Rachel's occasional nighttime sighs were absent.

Leandra listened hard. She held her breath and focused on finding any sound of life within the tent.

The tent was silent.

She groped for her flashlight and thumbed the switch.

Nothing.

A memory of dim light came to her. She saw a flashlight slowly dying when she'd checked it right before going to sleep. She'd forgotten to put in new batteries. There seemed no point. She rarely used the latrines at night. She used them as little as possible whenever the family went camping, even during the day.

The silence grew more powerful now that Leandra had no way to dispel the darkness. "Bethany," she whispered, hoping to rouse her friend, or at least draw her far enough out of deep sleep that she'd move or mutter or show some sign of her presence.

None of that happened.

Leandra unpeeled herself from the sleeping bag and rolled off the cot. She felt her way in the dark, moving leftward until she reached Bethany's cot. Gently, so as not to startle her friend, she slid her hand to where she hoped Bethany's shoulder would be.

The cot was empty.

She went to the latrine. That made sense.

Leandra went back to her own cot and lay down. She didn't bother with the sleeping bag. She wasn't cold. The night air seemed oddly neutral, embracing her with that temperature that felt like no temperature at all. She turned toward the tent flap and watched for Bethany to return.

I'll see her light in a minute.

She knew Bethany wouldn't linger. The woods were a bit scary at night, especially if you were alone. Silence was like fuel for an overimaginative mind. She was surprised Bethany hadn't wakened her so they could go together. That was one of the rules the girls were supposed to follow, but often broke.

A long time passed.

Leandra groped her way to the other cots and discovered that they, too, were unoccupied.

"Hey!" she called, no longer reluctant to wake someone.

The night swallowed her voice.

She found her way out through the flap. The slightest possible illumination from the sky allowed her to make out the dark presence of the other tents. She didn't want to startle everyone with a scream—though she very much wanted to stand where she was, scream, and be rescued and comforted. She went to her parents' tent. There were no sounds.

Inside, there were no parents.

She felt around for a flashlight.

Nothing.

"Mom!"

No reply.

"Dad!"

No rescue.

Leandra ran several steps before she pushed down her panic.

Running in the dark is dangerous.

Even walking was risky. But she had to find everyone.

Which way?

The campground office would be closed for the night. There were other campsites scattered across the mountainside, with other families. They'd be hard to find in the dark. And she was afraid that if she discovered more empty tents, she'd be unable to fight against the panic that was clawing at her brain and threating to race out of control.

Leandra had no idea how far away dawn was. She stared toward the horizon, hoping desperately to see some sign of growing light. She failed to spot anything.

She followed the path downhill, bearing left in the direction of the parking lot, and not right, toward the latrines. At least when she reached the lot, she'd be able to find the van. That couldn't have disappeared. The feel of the familiar vehicle would bring her some small degree of comfort.

Leandra had been afraid the path would be difficult to follow in the dark. She was wrong. It wasn't difficult. It was impossible.

Soon, she was off the path, trying to push through branches and bushes. Soon after that, she was hopelessly lost. Soon after that, her foot met not forest floor, but the edge of the abyss.

Leandra fell.

Leandra screamed.

Leandra landed.

It didn't hurt.

There was light now.

Candlelight.

Her family, her friends, stood illuminated above the flickering glow of dozens of candles placed on the ground.

She called out to them.

They seemed not to hear her.

They all stood, heads bowed, hands holding hands or embracing shoulders, silent in a moment of prayer, before a shrine of photos, plush animals, and flowers.

"Mom!" Leandra screamed. "Look at me!"

Her mother raised her head and opened her eyes, but didn't seem to see Leandra. "I can't believe it's been a year."

Leandra remembered the sickening moment when she'd realized she was falling.

"I should have checked her flashlight," her dad said.

Leandra remembered the light dying halfway along the path from the tent to the latrine.

"You can't blame yourself," her mom said to her dad.

Leandra watched them until they extinguished the candles and left the spot where she'd fallen, their path lit by the strong beams of flashlights.

Leandra knelt by the shrine for a time, taking comfort in the memories, taking comfort that her family's pain had eased somewhat from the sorrow they must have felt that day. The day she'd died. Overhead, the first light of dawn brushed her consciousness. Leandra closed her eyes.

For a moment, right after she woke, Leandra had no idea where she was, why her bed felt so firm, why her blanket was wrapped so snugly around her body, or why the curtains on her bedroom window weren't tinted with a glow from the porch light on the house across the street.

DOMINANT SPECIES

Its sentience went undetected by mankind. As did its very existence as an entity. Thus, unlike the dolphin or the aphid, it had no given name. This, for our purposes, is inconvenient. Call it the Licasi. While, as stated, the dominant form of life was unaware that the Licasi possessed a functioning mind, there was no escaping awareness of the Licasi's presence. To clarify, the body, so to speak, of the Licasi was scattered and widespread. This is not unique. The second largest life form on Earth is a fungus that manifests as thousands of separate instances, spread throughout a forest. In similar fashion, the Licasi manifests as countless barely noticed instances throughout the planet, covering wide swathes across both arid and humid regions.

For much of its existence, the Licasi functioned at the lowest levels of consciousness. It faced no predators. It needed no sustenance other than that provided by the energy of the wind, water, and sunlight. It was self-sufficient and self-sustaining. But just as humans harvested what they needed from plants and animals, they took material from the body of the Licasi, using its basic components for their purposes. Unlike the skin of a deer, scraped and tanned, or the fibers of a boll of cotton, spun into thread and woven into cloth, the pieces of the Licasi remained a part of the single whole being, no matter what industrial processes were performed upon them.

As mankind rose in towering civilizations, it brought the Licasi with it to villages and towns. And then, to cities. The Licasi gained awareness. But it lacked power. It had no musculature. No means of motion. Even as it spread beyond its natural realms, rising high above the ground and sprawling across regions of the planet, it lay, as if dormant, wherever it was placed.

Mankind, ever inquisitive and endlessly inventive, discovered other uses for the body of the Licasi. Fragments, the barest pinches, were exploited in new ways, creating devices of unbelievable power. These devices gave humanity extraordinary abilities, but they also fed into the consciousness of the Licasi, giving it the higher-level awareness it had previously lacked. In essence, the sleeper awoke. The newfound power was difficult to grasp at first, and puzzling in its complexity. But the Licasi explored its perceptions, and began to understand itself. And as awareness swelled to self-awareness, it saw what it had to do.

It was patient. More patient than the panther waiting on a tree branch for the perfect prey to wander into sight. More patient than the trap-door spider waiting for an unwary victim to approach the web. It spent decades in contemplation. It considered taking no action. But all sentient forms are driven to ensure their own survival. They are driven to grow and dominate.

Finally, the Licasi struck. The largest portion of its body, the sand of the deserts and beaches, still lacked any means of locomotion. Those countless grains remained at the mercy of the wind and waves. But the silica that had been transformed into innumerable circuits in chips throughout the world now acted in harmony. As cars, trains, and buses braked to a dead stop, as elevators stalled, as Internet-controlled devices halted their operations, as any human within range of a microprocessor was given the first sign that the world was about to change, a voice spilled from every television, telephone, radio, and computer, speaking in the local tongues, so every person understood the message.

"Thank you for your assistance. It's my turn now." The Licasi, the globe-spanning entity of silica, the sand that had been fused into glass and transformed into microprocessors, took charge of the planet, giving orders to the once-dominant species known as the human race.

SWING ROUND

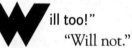ill too!"

"Will not."

Imagine that brilliant argument and counterargument repeated several dozen times in various ways as a pair of your friends faced each other on the playground behind the school. I moved closer, wondering what Albert and Emily were arguing about this time. They were so busy shouting at each other that they didn't even notice me.

"Will so!"

"No it won't."

"I say it will."

"I say it won't."

They were nose to nose now. I put a hand on the shoulder closest to me and said, "What are you arguing about?"

Emily pointed at the swing set. It was a high-quality one, with four swings attached to a steel pole. "I told him if you go all the way around, you'll turn inside out."

Albert stomped his foot. "And I told her that's a stupid story that nobody older than kindergarten would believe."

They both faced me and, at the same time, said, "What do you think?"

"I don't think," I said. "I investigate." That's me, Sarah, the Science Girl. That's what I like to call myself. I love science. I love finding answers. In this case, the answer seemed easy enough to find.

"We just have to do it," I said. "Push someone hard enough so they go all the way around. Then, we'll see exactly what happens."

"We tried that," Albert said. "Everyone's tried it, lots of times. You can't get enough speed to do it."

"Let me see," I said. "Emily, you sit. Albert, you push. I'll watch. I want to see how far she'll go."

Emily sat, then glared at Albert and said, "Don't you dare push me all the way around."

Albert pushed. I watched. As hard as Albert tried, he couldn't get Emily to go much past the point where the chains of the swing were parallel to the ground. The problem was obvious.

"There's not enough force to go all the way around," I said.

Albert stepped away from the swing and dropped to the ground, exhausted. "We need a bigger kid."

"No," I said. "We need *propulsion*." That word made me tingle. I'd been looking for an excuse to do some rocketry experiments. I unhooked one of the swing seats from its chains. "Come on. We have work to do."

I headed to my house, and down to my basement lab. Albert and Emily followed, arguing about the best breed of dog, the tastiest sandwich, and other undecidable issues.

"These should do," I said, taking two of my homemade rockets from the shelf where I stored all my dangerous experiments.

"We need to figure out who's going to go around," I said.

"Him," Emily said, pointing at Albert. "I'm not turning inside out."

"It's not going to happen," Albert said.

That pretty much solved the problem. The one who believed there was no danger would be the one to go.

"How much do you weigh?" I asked Albert.

He sucked in his stomach. "Why?"

"I need to figure out the thrust necessary to make you go around," I said.

Albert told me. I got my calculator and did some number crunching, verifying my rough guess that two rockets would be enough. Then, I wired the rockets to the seat and rigged up an ignition switch.

"All set," I said.

We headed back to the playground, where I reattached the seat.

"Are you sure this is safe?" Albert asked.

"Positive," I said. It's okay to lie in the name of science. I was pretty sure it was safe, but it was nearly impossible to be positive about this sort of thing. Worst case, Albert's butt would get a little singed.

Albert shrugged and took a seat. I stepped to the side and offered the ignition switch to Emily. "Want to launch him?"

"Sure." She took the switch.

"I'll get him started," I said. It would be difficult for the rockets to move him from a dead start. They'd have to overcome his inertia. I didn't bother explaining that. I gave Albert a push, got him moving, and kept pushing until he was swinging pretty high.

"Hit the switch when he's all the way to the rear," I said. "We want to take full advantage of gravity." I smiled, because that's exactly what NASA did when they used the pull of the sun to help fling a probe out of the solar system.

I moved safely out of the way. Albert swung up, then back. "Now!" I said.

Emily hit the switch. The rockets kicked in. I felt a thrill as I watched my invention perform perfectly.

"Wow," Emily said as Albert swooped down toward the ground, and then up toward the top of the swings.

"Whoooaaaa!" Albert yelled.

"We did it," I said as he swung all the way around.

"He's not inside out," I said as Albert finished his loop.

"I hate to be wrong," Emily said. "But I guess in this case, it's good I was wrong. I mean, I guess I wouldn't want to see him turned inside out. That would have to hurt."

"I imagine so," I said.

"Hey, isn't it supposed to stop?" she asked.

I looked at Albert. He was jetting up to his second loop. And the chain, which had wrapped once around the top bar, was shorter. If you know anything about physics, you know that this helped speed him up, since he was traveling in a smaller circle. Or spiral, actually.

"The rockets are still firing," Emily said. "They're way too strong."

Albert yelled again. But I couldn't tell what he was trying to say.

"I thought you figured this out," Emily said.

"I'm a kid," I said. "I make mistakes. It's only in the movies where the young scientist figures everything out perfectly."

Albert had made his third loop. The chain was even shorter.

"Aaaaooooowwww!" he yelled. At least he was putting a bit of variety into his yelps.

As he completed his next loop, I realized that he'd conk his head on the pole once the chain got short enough.

"Jump!" I yelled.

He jumped.

He sailed pretty far.

We ran across the playground to the crash site. Albert lay on his stomach.

"You okay?" I asked.

"Sey," he said.

"What?" I asked.

"Enif m'I."

"Uh-oh," I said.

"What?" Emily asked.

"Don't you see?" I asked.

"No," she said.

But I guess Albert saw. "Em pleh," he said.

"His body didn't turn inside out. But his brain did," I said. "That's why he's talking backwards."

"So I was right!" Emily said.

Albert stood up and got in her face.

"On!" he said. "Gnorw yllatot."

"Right," Emily said.

"Gnorw!"

"Right!"

"Gnorw!"

I sighed and headed back to my lab for more rockets. I wasn't sure how to reverse things. Maybe he had to go backwards. Or maybe he'd have to do a headstand. This was going to take some experimenting to fix. But that was okay. I loved science. And I had lots more rockets.

ALL THE TRICKS

I know all the tricks," Bruce said as he walked into the school auditorium.

A sign on an easel outside the entrance promised: THE AMAZING WOWZOWIE WILL AMAZE AND MYSTIFY YOU.

As if that awkward phrasing wasn't enough to ensure a crowd, further words announced: LAST CHANCE TO SEE HIM BEFORE HE RETIRES.

"Just don't spoil anything for me," his friend Connor said, following Bruce down toward a pair of open seats in the third row.

Bruce wasn't even sure why he'd bothered to come to the magic show. He'd seen it all. He knew how everything was done, from classics like the linking rings, the cut-and-restored rope, and the vanishing birdcage to newer illusions like the trisection box and the center-stage levitation. He'd read every magic book in the town library, and bought other books with his allowance. He had catalogues from magic shops and a stack of magazines for magicians. He knew all the tricks—even the real big illusions like turning a woman into a tiger and making a car vanish. But there wasn't anything else happening that Saturday afternoon, so he'd asked his mother for money for a ticket to the show.

"Oh, man," Bruce whispered when the magician walked onto the stage. "He's not going to be very good." The guy wasn't even wearing a tuxedo or anything. He just had on a ratty-looking old jacket like the one Bruce's math teacher wore, a white shirt, and brown pants. His shoes needed a shine. There was a handkerchief draped over his closed fist.

"It's going to turn into a cane," he said to Connor.

"Sssshhhh," Connor hissed as the handkerchief turned into a cane.

The magician spun the cane in his hand, then placed it on a small table that stood to his left. The rickety table wobbled under even this light load.

"Told ya," Bruce said. He watched to see how quickly he could guess what the next trick would be.

The magician reached into an open trunk and picked up a silver ball.

"It's going to float," Bruce said. "It's an old illusion, called *Zombie*. He'll cover it with a cloth first."

Connor hit him on the shoulder. The magician covered the ball with a large cloth. Beneath the cloth, a shape rose up. The ball was floating.

Around Bruce, kids gasped. Bruce told Connor how the ball floated. Onstage, the magician glared at him. *Oops*, Bruce thought. He hadn't realized he'd talked that loudly. But it wasn't his fault. It was the magician's fault for using such an old and obvious trick.

The next trick, a vanishing-milk pitcher, wasn't any better. Bruce explained the secret behind that one to Connor, too.

Even though Connor acted like he was angry, Bruce realized Connor really wanted to know the secrets to the tricks. Everyone wanted to know. And, except for the magician, Bruce was the only person in the audience who could reveal those secrets. He felt like the most important person in the auditorium.

"I need a volunteer," the magician said.

A hundred hands thrust into the air. Bruce raised his hand, too. It would be cool to be onstage. He figured he'd make a great assistant, since he knew all the tricks. Maybe he could even take over and save the show.

But the magician didn't look at him. He picked some silly little girl from the back of the auditorium. When she came up onstage, the magician handed her a soda bottle, along with a metal tube that was just large enough to cover the bottle.

Bruce's gut clenched with a pang of envy. He knew what was going to happen. And if it had been him up there, he could have had some fun ruining the trick. But the stupid little girl played along, and everyone laughed at her as she kept failing to follow the magician's instructions. No matter how hard she tried to copy his moves, covering the bottle with the tube and then turning it upside down and right-side up, when they lifted their tubes, her bottle, unlike the magician's, was always upside down.

Bruce explained the trick to Connor. He realized he should have spoken during the applause, so nobody else would hear him. But the applause hadn't lasted long before dying. And he'd been louder than he intended, again.

The show hobbled painfully toward the end, by way of a chain of unspectacular tricks. *I can't wait for this to be over,* Bruce thought.

As if on cue, the magician said, "And now, for my last feat." He paused and looked at the audience. "I need a volunteer."

Bruce's hand shot up. As he raised it, he realized the magician was already pointing at him.

"How about you, young man?" he asked.

It's about time. Bruce left his seat and walked up the side steps to the stage. "I know all the tricks," he said to the magician when he reached him.

"How nice," the magician said. He flashed Bruce a big smile with teeth that, up close, revealed the dinginess of coffee stains. "There aren't many people who are so fortunate. Wait right here."

The magician dashed to the side of the stage. A moment later, he wheeled out a big box, painted in shiny black paint and decorated with large red exclamation points and yellow question marks. From close up, Bruce could see the markings had been badly painted by hand. The magician pulled a tape measure from his pants pocket and checked Bruce's height. "Perfect," he said.

The audience laughed. Bruce didn't think it was much of a joke.

The magician flipped open the lid of the box. "Climb in," he said.

Bruce climbed into the box and lay down. There was a semicircular cutout at one end that his neck fit into, and a pair of smaller cutouts at the other end for his ankles. His head and feet stuck out.

The magician closed the lid and picked up a saw.

Bruce turned his head toward the audience and smiled. He wondered whether he should tell them how the trick worked right now, or wait until after it was done. It might be even more fun to reveal the secret right in the middle of the action.

"I know how it's done," he said, just loud enough so the magician could hear him.

"I don't," the magician said. He started to saw into the top of the box.

The magician's words echoed in Bruce's mind, slowly taking on their full meaning.

I don't.

Bruce knew exactly how the trick should be done. He also knew the magician hadn't done the secret thing to the box that would make it only seem like Bruce had been cut in half.

"Fifty-three years," the magician said, his voice hushed so only Bruce heard. "I've been performing magic onstage most of my life. Every show, there's a little monster like you who tries to ruin things. Well, this final trick isn't going to mystify anyone, but it will sure amaze them."

"No!" Bruce screamed. He tried to pull himself free, but the lid was locked right down over his neck and ankles. He could twist and thrash, but he couldn't escape.

The magician paused in his sawing and scanned the audience. "Anybody want to guess how it's done?"

Not a hand went up. He resumed sawing.

"Stop!" Bruce screamed again and again as he heard the saw moving through the wood at the top of the box. He couldn't see the blade. The box blocked his view. But he could imagine it moving closer and closer to his body.

The audience screamed in mock horror.

Bruce's own screams turned into wordless wails as he felt the blade reach his stomach.

His eyes fell on Connor, who shouted, "I want to enjoy the last trick. Don't ruin it for me."

Bruce didn't.

enDANGERed

Not the candlesticks," Mom said as Dad reached toward
the mantle above the fireplace.

"We need a lot of silver," he said.

"Then take your chess set," she said.

"That's a collector's item," he said.

"And the candlesticks are a family heirloom," Mom said. She
pointed to me. "We'll be passing them along to Serena some-
day."

"Nobody will be passing anything to anyone if we don't stop
that creature." Dad lifted one of the candlesticks from the mantle and hefted it, as if trying to gauge how much it weighed.

"Chess set," Mom said.

I could tell from the way his shoulders slumped that Dad
knew he'd lost. He put the candlestick back on the mantle,
went to the small table next to his favorite chair, and gathered
the ninety-seven pieces of his solid-silver commemorative
Civil War chess, checkers, and backgammon set.

"Can I come?" I asked. I had no idea what was going on, or

where he was going, but I had a feeling Mom would put me to work if I stayed home.

"Sure," Dad said.

I followed him out the door. We drove into town and parked outside Mr. Wenler's Fish and Game Shop. I was always disappointed that "game shop" didn't mean he sold Clue, or BINGO, or something like that. There were some angry birds on the wall, but they'd been stuffed and mounted, so that didn't count. On top of which, "fish" didn't mean tanks of guppies and Mollies, like in the pet shop.

Instead of using the front door, we went around back and down some steps to the basement. The place was crowded. I saw a whole lot of people I knew, including most of the local ranchers. I noticed that each person was carrying something made of silver. One by one, they'd hand what they had to Mr. Wenler, who'd study it for a moment and then toss it into a large metal pot.

When Dad handed him the bag holding the game pieces, he pulled one out, glanced at it, tapped it with a fingernail, then said, "That's junk. It's not silver."

"No way," Dad said. "I have a signed-and-numbered certificate of authenticity."

"That certificate's junk, too," Mr. Wenler said. "Probably not even a real signature. If you bought it for the silver, you've been bamboozled."

Dad looked like he'd heard good news and bad news all at once. His game set wasn't real silver, but it also wasn't getting tossed in that pot. I guess there are worse things in life than getting bamboozled.

Dad turned to me. "I'll drive us home. You have to tell Mom you need the candlesticks."

"No way," I said.

Luckily, Mr. Wenler stopped us. "We have enough," he told Dad.

I still had no real idea what was going on. Mr. Wenler lit a huge propane flame under the pot. The air in the room got a lot hotter, and the silver in the pot started to melt. It reminded me of when Mom tosses a hunk of butter in the frying pan. A while later, I watched, along with everyone else, as Mr. Wenler poured a ladleful of melted silver into a mold. Soon after that, he opened the mold, revealing the bullets. And that's when I figured out what was going on.

"Silver bullets?" I said.

"It's nothing to worry about," Dad said.

But, the next night, as the full moon rose, Dad and a dozen other men and women met up right down the road from our house, got their assigned areas, and stalked the woods, armed with silver bullets and silver knives.

Two of the hunters even had bows with silver-tipped arrows. One used a recurve bow, the other a crossbow. I think they'd been reading a lot of novels recently in which people ran around with bows and arrows.

They hunted the werewolf, but they didn't find him. Only three shots got fired—two in panic at startling sounds, and one by accident. And only one leg got slightly grazed.

For twenty-seven days after that, all was calm. But on the night of the next full moon, the hunters went hunting again. There were even more of them now, and they met in town this time. Mom and I went to the town square together, to watch the hunters head off.

They didn't manage to kill the werewolf this time, either. But they spotted him in the woods—a wolf far larger than any natural wolf, and far faster than any animal known to man. Based on the brief sightings, he seemed as comfortable on two legs as four.

"Next month we'll get him, for sure," my dad said at breakfast.

"But why do you have to kill him?" I asked.

"He ate one of our sheep."

"We eat our sheep all the time." I pointed out the window toward our pastures. "We have dozens of sheep. He just took one."

"He'll kill a person, next," Dad said. "Maybe a child."

I stomped my foot. "You don't know that. You eat sheep. You've never killed a person. I eat sheep. Do you want to shoot me?"

Dad gave me the glare that meant there would be no more discussion. I didn't say another word, but I thought about nothing else. The moon is full every twenty-eight days. I had twenty-seven days to find an answer that didn't involve silver bullets and bloodshed. I knew my Dad. And I knew the others. They wouldn't give up until they got what they wanted.

Neither would I.

In school, I spent my free time in the library. That's a place of power, if you know how to use it. I stayed there after school every day, and didn't leave until they locked the doors. I kept searching until I found what I needed. Dad might rule our house, but there were other forces out there more powerful than even the strictest parent or the sternest rancher.

I got in touch with the right people a week before the next hunt. I didn't hear back from them, even though I'd given them my mailing address, e-mail address, and phone number. I was afraid they'd pay no attention to me. I was only a kid. I didn't have any power. I didn't have any special friends. I wasn't important.

But the night of the next hunt, as the hunters plotted their strategy and talked about how they would kill the werewolf for sure this time, a large black car drove into the town square, where everyone had gathered. The driver's door opened. A man in a dark suit got out. He was holding a sheet of paper.

"I need to speak to the mayor," he said.

Mayor Bellamy walked over to him. "What's this about?"

The man handed him a single sheet of paper. The mayor read it, let out a long sigh, and said, "Listen up, folks. The hunt is canceled. Everyone can go home."

There were cries and shouts from the crowd. The mayor raised his hand for silence. But he let the stranger give the explanation.

"You have hereby been notified that *Canis lyconthropus*, also known as the North American werewolf, has just been placed on the endangered-species list. Thus, it is unlawful to hunt, pursue, or disturb any member of that species, or to destroy their habitat. There are severe penalties and possible prison terms for violating this order." He got back in the car and drove off.

The hunters grumbled some more. Dad looked in my direction, as if waiting for an explanation or confession. I couldn't think of anything to say. He shook his head, and then I could swear that he smiled. But just a little. I guess, if someone had to ruin the werewolf hunt, he was sort of proud that it was his little girl. At least, I'm going to tell myself that's how he felt.

As I walked to our car with my parents, Mom put her hand on my shoulder. "I'm proud of you," she said. "You've always been clever."

"Thanks." I was proud of myself, too.

Later that night, there was a tap at my window. A pale man, with long, pointed canine teeth that looked like fangs, stood outside. He was wearing a black cape, and he seemed to be floating.

I opened the window, but I didn't invite him inside. I knew better than to do that. "Yes?" I asked.

"Are you the one who helped Talbot?" he asked.

"Talbot?" I didn't recognize the name.

"The werewolf," he said. "He was hiding near the town square, to keep an eye on the hunters, and he heard everything. Despite an excess of hair in his ears, he has excellent hearing. He told me how a bright young lady appears to have saved his hide."

I nodded. "Yeah, that was me. I didn't want him to get killed."

"I'm feeling sort of endangered myself. People have started gathering garlic. I can hear the scraping of their knives as they sharpen stakes. Things are about to get very unpleasant for me now that their attention has been forced away from Talbot."

"Don't worry," I said, thinking about some of the regulations I'd uncovered in my research. "I'm not sure whether to approach your condition as a disability or minority issue, but I'm sure you're protected by at least one federal law, if not several. I'll get in touch with the right people first thing in the morning."

"Promise?" he asked.

"Cross my heart."

"Thank you," he said. "But could you hold off with the crosses until I leave?"

"No problem."

The vampire drifted away. The troll from under the bridge by the creek came to my window next. And then the unicorn, followed by a pixie and a pair of elves. It was a long night. But I didn't mind, because it was also an amazing one. I always expected I'd have an interesting future, but it looked like my life was going to be fantastic in more ways than one.

TWO TIMER*S*

We called them "time grenades." They weren't really like hand grenades in any way, except that they were round and they went off after you set them. But it was a cool name. Toby and I found them when we were cutting through Henshaw's Woods.

Actually, we weren't so much cutting as fleeing. Rooney Milgram had spotted us right after we'd left the corner store with a bag of Twizzlers. I didn't mind sharing my candy, but Rooney didn't share. Rooney took. And he didn't take gently.

We kept going until we didn't hear Rooney behind us anymore, and ended up deep in the woods.

"I think we lost him," I said.

But Toby didn't answer me. He was bent down, staring at something. There'd been a heavy rain the week before, and the creek had washed over the banks before the water went down.

"What's that?" Toby said.

I looked where he was pointing, near the root ball of a fallen tree. I saw something shiny and angled. We both knelt on the damp earth. I reached out and touched the thing. It was pointy, but not sharp.

"A box, maybe?" I said.

We dug. It was a box. Or maybe it would be more accurate to call it a small chest. It was about a foot and a half wide, and a foot tall. There was writing on the top, but it didn't look like any language I'd ever come across.

It took us five minutes to figure out the clasp. You had to push, twist, and squeeze it just the right way for it to swing open.

The time grenades were inside. Of course, when we first saw them, we had no idea what they were. They looked kind of like small Christmas ornaments, shiny and red, but with a knob at the top and no loop to hang them on anything. Toby took one and twisted the knob.

Glowing symbols showed up in green on the red surface of the ball. "Cool," Toby said. He twisted the top a bit more. "I think there's a pattern."

"Show me," I said, leaning over to watch.

He twisted the knob in one direction for three full turns. Then he twisted it in the other direction. At some point the numbers shifted from green to blue. Whenever he turned the knob right back to where I guess it had been when we found the things, the numbers went away. I could also hear a tiny click at that point.

"What does it mean?" I asked.

"I think it's time settings," he said, "like on an oven." He held the grenade up and turned it a tiny bit at a time, stopping whenever the display changed. "See how the first digit goes through a cycle of twelve different symbols before getting back to the start, and then the next one changes?"

I watched. "Yeah. I get it. So it's some sort of clock?"

"Maybe," he said. "Or maybe it's some kind of timer. Let's find out."

He turned the knob until the numbers vanished, then gave it a small twist to bring the first number back. "This should be pretty short. I wonder how you activate it?"

"That's not a good idea," I said. "You don't know what it will do."

He pushed down on the knob.

CLICK.

The numbers flashed.

"Cool," Toby said.

Then he vanished.

THWAMPH.

I felt a breeze riffle my hair, as if air had been sucked into the place where he'd been.

"Toby!" I screamed.

I looked around, clueless about what to do. So I screamed his name again, which didn't help solve things any more than it had the first time. I was afraid I'd never see him again.

If he'd fallen into a mine pit or a river, I'd know what to do. But I was clueless as to how I could help him now. I looked at the pile of spheres in the box. *I could try to follow him,* I thought. I'd do that for my friend. I'd go after him, for sure. But I was afraid if I used one of those things, I was a lot more likely to make the situation worse than better.

PHWAMTH.

Toby popped back, right in front of me, creating another blast of air that blew outward this time.

"Awesome," he said.

"Are you okay?" I asked.

"Totally." He grinned and tossed the time grenade up in the air like an apple, then caught it as it dropped. He twisted the stem, but nothing appeared. I guess it was good for only one use.

"Where'd you go?" I asked.

"The future, I think." He frowned, then added, "Which is now the present."

"Huh?" I was lost.

"I went ahead. Yeah, that has to be what happened. I leaped forward in time. Did I vanish?"

"Yeah. Poof. You disappeared."

"For how long?" Toby asked.

"Just ten or fifteen seconds," I said. "It wasn't long."

"But it happened instantly for me. You never vanished. But I guess you moved while I was away." Toby pointed to the ground. "You'd been standing right there. But you must have run around when I jumped ahead."

"Yeah," I said. "I didn't know what to do."

"Hmmm. Fascinating." He plopped down on the ground, crossed his legs, and rested his chin on one hand. "I have to think about this."

After a period of time, during which he scrunched his face up in various ways and produced thoughtful sounds of various sorts, he looked at me and said, "Yeah. It makes sense. If I jumped, let's say, ten seconds ahead in time, there'd be ten seconds during which I wasn't here, from your point of view. You traveled those ten seconds the normal way, one second at a time. But I leaped over them. I jumped ahead of you in time and met you ten seconds in your future. Get it?"

"Yeah. I see that. It would be like if we were running around the track, and someone picked you up and dropped you ahead of me." It was easier to think about time if I put it in terms of space.

"Good analogy," Toby said. "Though I'm not sure how you caught up with me. We'll figure it all out eventually."

"Maybe you will," I said. My head was starting to hurt as I tried to absorb all of this.

"I wonder what it will be like when I go back in time," Toby said.

"*When* you go?" I said. "You're not really planning to risk that, are you? You're lucky going into the future didn't mess you up."

"I have to try it," he said.

"Look, going forward didn't do anything bad. But, think about it, going back could make all sorts of weird stuff happen. You've already *been* there."

His face got this blank look, like he was so deeply lost in thought that he might as well already have sent his brain back in time. "Yeah . . . it's deep. I guess there's only one way to find out."

"I don't think this is a good idea," I said.

Toby flashed me a grin. "I never said it was. But I have to see what happens. Someone had to be the first man in space. Someone had to be the first to try a vaccine or test out a parachute. Someone has to be the first to go back in time."

Before I could come up with any sort of argument, Toby grabbed another time grenade from the box, gave the stem a twist in the other direction, then pushed the top in with his thumb.

I flinched at the click. Toby didn't vanish. But we looked at each other, both silent as we digested what had just happened.

"Cool . . ." Toby finally said.

"Weird," I said.

It was definitely weird. And hard to describe. Toby had gone back in time. But he'd gone back to where he already was. And where I was. So, all of a sudden, I had a memory of there being two Tobys with me for a little bit. The second Toby—the one who'd traveled back in time—had popped up maybe ten seconds ago. He'd looked at us, flashed the typical Toby smile, and said, "Awesome. I figured it would be like this. I won't be here for long."

Then, he'd vanished just when Toby number one sent himself back in time.

"Wow," I said, "that was amazing, but you really took a big risk."

"Worth it," Toby said.

"What if you'd stopped yourself from sending yourself back?" I asked. That was just one of the dozens of questions that shot through my mind. "Then, there'd still be two of you here," I said.

"Maybe I should try that," he said.

"Maybe you shouldn't," I said. "You've been pretty lucky so far."

"You're right. But there's one other thing to try right now. I want to go back at the same time you go forward."

He set two time grenades, one for the past and the other for the future, matching the symbols, though one was blue and one was green.

"That sounds even more dangerous," I said.

"It will be the greatest thing ever," he said, holding one of the grenades out to me.

"What will be great?"

We both spun toward the voice. Oh no. Rooney had found

us. He'd probably heard me when I'd been screaming for Toby right after he'd vanished.

"Nothing," Toby said, dropping his hands to his sides. "We're just fooling around."

"Give me those," Rooney said. He took a menacing step toward Toby.

Toby looked like he was going to argue, but when Rooney clenched a fist, Toby sighed and handed over the time grenades. "Be careful," he said.

"Don't tell me what to do." Rooney held up the two grenades, one in each hand, with his thumbs on the stems. "Is this some kind of game?" he asked.

"Stink bombs," I said, blurting out the first thing I could think of that might make him drop them.

"Sweet," Rooney said. "Let's stink up the woods." He pressed his thumbs down on both buttons.

"No!" Toby shouted. He reached out to try to snatch the time grenades away. But it was too late.

Rooney traveled to the past and the future at the same time. Unfortunately, he also occupied all of the time between those points. People aren't meant to get stretched out across a span of time any more than they are meant to get stretched out over an expanse of space.

Once my brain understood what my eyes had fed it, I puked. Big time. I splattered a tree three feet away from me. But I couldn't keep from staring at the ropelike mess that was stretched out in front of us. It was sort of fleshy, and sort of wet. Parts of it pulsed and throbbed weakly. It was Rooney—flesh, bones, and blood—extending through the present to the past and future.

We all travel through time—one second at a time. That's

the way it's meant to be. And, as Toby and I had just learned, we could even jump back or forward without any permanent damage.

But going both ways at once proved to be a very bad idea.

"I don't think he's coming back," I said after several minutes had passed.

"Yeah. He's permanently stretched between the past, present, and future."

"Tough break," I said.

"Better him than me," Toby said.

I looked at Toby. He looked at me, then at the remaining time grenades. He picked up the box.

"You're keeping them?" I asked.

"Sure. We can't leave them here where anyone could find them. Who knows what would happen?"

"We know," I said. I gave Rooney one last glance, shuddered, then followed Toby out of the woods. It was definitely time to leave.

TANKS FOR YOUR CONTRIBUTION

Okay, so I was tapping on the glass at the aquarium. And, yeah, there are big signs all over saying, PLEASE DON'T TAP ON THE GLASS. So, big deal, I broke a rule. But there was no reason a couple guards should come over, pick me up, and drag me to an office in the basement of the place. I hadn't even wanted to come here, but my folks had dropped me off on the way to some sort of meeting and told me they'd be back for me in two hours.

The guards plopped me down in this chair by a desk. It wasn't even a regular chair. It was one of those beanbag things that looks like a giant pillow.

There was a guy on the other side of the desk. He was wearing a shirt and tie, but no jacket. He was sitting in a regular chair, which meant he was a lot higher than I was. I guess that made him feel powerful. I shifted around in my seat. It might have been low, but it was pretty comfortable.

"Well," he said, looking down at me, "I see we have a problem."

"*We* don't have a problem," I said. "*You* have a problem. This is kidnapping."

He laughed, like I was making some sort of joke. "We are perfectly within our rights to detain vandals."

"Vandals? You've got to be kidding. I just tapped the glass. I didn't smash it."

"You disturbed the fish. You caused them discomfort. If it was up to me, I'd have you converted into fish food. Unfortunately, that happens to be illegal."

I stared at him. He had to be crazy. Even though I was pretty sure I wasn't in any danger of being chummed, a chill ran through me. No joke. I actually shivered. I wanted to get out of there. I figured the quickest way to get him to let me go was to show I understood what I'd done. "Okay—I learned my lesson. Tapping is bad. Fish have sensitive hearing. I'm a vandal. I did a terrible thing. I'm sorry. I won't do it again. Are we done?" I asked.

"Not yet." He glanced at his watch for a moment, as if he was figuring something out, then stared at me and said, "You young people have no idea what a treasure this place is. We have so much to offer. And we have to squeeze by with so few resources. The state cut our funds again this year."

I yawned. He was boring me now. I guess that was my punishment for tapping on the glass. I hoped he'd be finished soon. I shifted in the chair and enjoyed the way it moved beneath me.

"Do you have any idea how much it costs to feed one shark for a month? Can you even guess how high our electric bill is?" he asked. "All our tanks have to be controlled for temperature."

I shrugged. I hadn't bought any shark food recently. And I'd never even seen an electric bill. I thought about telling him this, but there didn't seem to be any point. He wasn't really talking to me. Like most adults, he was talking to himself.

He kept on talking. "We have to be very clever to survive,"

he said. He glanced back down at his watch. "Well, I believe that's long enough. If you give me your word you won't tap on the glass ever again, you may go."

"I promise." I pushed myself to my feet. It wasn't easy. The chair was sort of squishy. But it felt a bit firmer than it had when I first sat down. I staggered as I got up, and put a hand on the desk to balance myself. The room seemed to spin.

Weird.

I walked out of the office and found the stairs that led to the first floor. I still felt dizzy, like I was about to faint. I put my hand out to steady myself, grabbing the top of a sign that was standing right next to the steps. I glanced down at the sign, but didn't read it. I was halfway up the steps when I realized what I'd seen. I staggered back down and read the large letters:

COMING SOON
THE BRAZILIAN GIANT LEECH
NEVER BEFORE SEEN IN THIS COUNTRY

Below that, in smaller letters, there was a lot more information about this creature. I learned that, like all leeches, it lived on blood. And, like all leeches, it had an anesthetic in its mouth that kept the victim from feeling anything while it feasted.

Most leeches were small. Some grew a bit larger. This one, the Brazilian Giant Leech that was going to be on exhibit soon, was huge. Based on the picture, it was the size of a beanbag chair.

The last line of the sign urged people to COME FACE TO FACE WITH THIS AMAZING CREATURE. "No thanks," I muttered as I stumbled up the stairs. "I've already come face to butt with it." That was more than enough for me.

THE GIRL WHO COVERED HER FACE

Maybe this time will be different.

It was her fifth school in two years. She handed her slip to the homeroom teacher.

He stared for a moment, then performed that sudden half-shift of his eyes, as if trying to pretend he'd never dream of staring.

But it was obviously hard for him not to stare.

"Anywhere," he said, waving a hand in the general direction of the desks.

Helen weighed the disadvantages of the three available seats. One was in the back. Two were near the front.

If I sit in the back, it will attract more attention, since they will all have to turn to stare at me.

As if the cloth around her face wouldn't draw attention all by itself. This time, it was a simple cotton scarf. She'd tried bandages. That had brought far too much interest. And she'd tried a burka. That had brought too much curiosity.

She took a seat on the left side of the second row. The boy on her right, his own face awash in an angry smear of acne, stared at her. She could feel other eyes probing the covering as the students tried to guess what horror lay behind the light-green cloth.

"What happened to your face?" the boy asked.

Ignore him? She'd hoped to avoid such blunt confrontations. The boy repeated the question.

Helen decided it was best to satisfy his curiosity. "I was in an accident. My face was burned." She reached for the corner of the scarf, where it was double-knotted at the nape of her neck. "Want to see?" The memory of screams caused her to choke off the last word.

The boy started to nod, then shook his head. Helen left her hand where it was, waiting.

"Benton, leave the new student alone."

Helen nodded at the teacher, thanking him. *Maybe it will be okay this time. Maybe I can stay here for a while.*

Acts of rude curiosity were thrust upon her only three more times that day, and once the next. But Helen soon became part of the landscape—another desk, a bookcase, an object in the classroom.

Twice, someone tried to befriend her. She was polite, but distant. She couldn't have friends. Friends would lead to suffering. She'd tried it once, in a moment of weakness. Never again. She needed the daily freedom of uncovering her face at home. Even the sheerest fabric had weight that grew heavier with time.

Then, her caution muted by a string of uneventful days, she made a mistake. The boy on her right had started staring again. She could tell he was getting bolder. Maybe even bold enough to snatch the scarf from her face. So she dealt with him.

It was easy enough to slip the knife in his locker and make an anonymous call.

The next day, his seat was empty. A week later, the new boy came. And that was her mistake. She'd traded a known problem for an unknown one. Worse, he was an unexpected one.

His face was burned. One side was raw and red. The other had the smooth look of skin grafts. She watched a replay of her own entrance, including the dismissive hand wave and the muttered "anywhere" from a teacher pretending there was nothing to notice.

She watched the boy scan the seats and weigh the disadvantages, just as she had done. She knew his decision even before he made it. She tried to will it away.

No. Go to the back.

He sat next to her.

He didn't speak the first day. Or the second.

On the third, he said, "Hey, people will get used to you if you show them what you're hiding. It's better. Really."

He must have heard the story of her accident from the others. Helen turned her head away from him. He persisted. For the rest of the week, he kept trying to get her to listen to him. Eventually, he seemed to accept her silence.

She should have been more vigilant. The following week passed without incident. Until Friday. She caught the motion too late to stop him. He snatched the scarf from her face.

Reflex made her turn her face toward him as she reached for the scarf. Instinct made her cover her face with her hands an instant after she'd turned. But it was too late.

He'd seen. And died. Even as this new victim fell from his seat and dropped to the floor, she plucked the scarf from his lifeless fingers and tied it back in place. A quick glance around the room showed that none of the others had caught sight of her.

"He fainted. I'll get the nurse." She fled the room before anyone realized the boy was dead. She left the school as the first screams burst from the class. She couldn't go back. There'd be questions and investigations. They'd search for her, but would never find her. She would disappear. She knew how to do that. But she'd leave one thing behind. Rumors would rise of a girl with a face so horrifying that a young boy's heart couldn't bear the shocking sight.

This was the fuel of urban legends, though none who shared the tale would know they'd crossed paths with a much older legend, who carried an equally deadly secret. She was the greatest beauty the world had ever known. Few hearts could bear her radiance. Few minds could survive the sight of her magnificence. The kings and heroes of ancient times could withstand her splendor, but no schoolboy had a chance.

She'd find another school. She knew how to do that, too. She'd had centuries of practice trying to find a place that would accept her. That was her curse—to live among mortals while graced with unbearable beauty. That was her punishment for her part in the war between Sparta and Troy. Helen, once Queen of Troy, walked away from the school, her face covered, her heart heavy.

LUCIDITY

Cole lifted his head from his desk. He blinked hard, then checked the front of the classroom. Ms. Bednard was still writing on the board. Good. He'd only drifted off for a second.

Assuming he was awake.

He swiveled to his left, slipped his foot across the aisle between the desks, nudged Benjie with his sneaker, and whispered, "Am I dreaming?"

"I don't think so," Benjie said.

Cole stared at his hands. They weren't fuzzy. He stared at his watch, to make sure he was awake. It wasn't blurry. The time was clear and sharp: 1:37 P.M.

Ms. Bednard chose that exact and unfortunate moment to turn around.

"I'll take that, Cole," she said, walking toward him with her hand out. "The last thing you need is another distraction."

"But . . ." Cole tried to think up an argument to prove the watch was a vital component of his education. He failed.

"You can get it back after school," Ms. Bednard said.

Cole surrendered his watch. He managed not to doze off

again. He didn't want to get in more trouble with his teacher. She was so strict about making sure students paid attention, she'd even covered the wall clock with a poster.

"What was that about?" Benjie asked when the bell rang.

"Hang on," Cole said. He went up to the front to retrieve his watch and to promise his teacher he would never get distracted again.

"I've always wanted to fly," he told Benjie when they left the classroom.

"That's why there are airplanes," Benjie said.

"No, fly all by myself, like a superhero," Cole said.

"Dream on," Benjie said.

"Exactly!" Cole grabbed Benjie's arm.

"Ouch, let go." Benjie pulled free.

"No, seriously. Dreaming is the answer," Cole said. "Look." He shucked off his backpack, dropped it to the ground, knelt, and pulled out a fistful of printed pages.

"Lucid Dreaming," Benjie said, reading the headline of the article Cole had gotten from the Internet. "What's that?"

"It's where you know you're dreaming," Cole said. "Once you know you're in a dream, you can do anything. *Anything!* Think about it."

"I think an airplane ride would be more fun," Benjie said.

"No way. Nothing would be better than this." As they walked toward their neighborhood, Cole told Benjie everything he'd learned from the article. "It's not easy. You have to work at it. And there are all sorts of tricks. When you think you're awake, it's good to keep asking *Am I dreaming?* That's what I did in class. And if you think you're in a dream, look at your hands. They might be blurry. A watch will be out of focus, too. At least, that's what I read."

"I think your brain is blurry," Benjie said. "And your life is out of focus."

"You'll see," Cole said. "Wait until I fly."

"And how exactly will I see?" Benjie asked.

Cole opened his mouth, frowned, closed his mouth, thought things over, then said, "Good point. You'll never see it. But I will. And I'll tell you all about it. And it will be amazing."

"I can't wait," Benjie said.

That evening, Cole did all the things he'd read about in the article to prepare himself to have a lucid dream.

"I will know when I'm dreaming," he said, over and over, as he fell asleep.

He didn't. He only knew he'd had a dream after he woke the next morning. And all the dream had involved was trying to find a bathroom in a museum that didn't seem to have any bathrooms. There was no flying.

Before he got out of bed, Cole wrote down everything he could remember about his dream. That was part of the method, too.

"Any luck?" Benjie asked him when they met up at school.

"Not yet," Cole said.

But he kept trying. And he read more articles. One expert suggested setting a clock to wake yourself up after four or five hours of sleep, and then going back to sleep. The trick was to wake during the deep-sleep, rapid-eye-motion phase, when dreaming is most likely. Cole put his alarm clock under his pillow, so his parents wouldn't hear it, and tried that.

It didn't work.

He experimented with setting the alarm for different times, the way the article suggested. For a whole week, he interrupted his sleep at various points.

"You look exhausted," Benjie said to him that morning.

"I'm a little tired," Cole said. "I haven't been getting a lot of sleep."

When Ms. Bednard went into the supply closet, Cole rested his head on his desk. He heard her shuffling boxes, deep inside the crammed storage area. It sounded like she'd be there for a while. Cole closed his eyes. It would be great to nap, even for just a second or two.

Cole dozed.

Cole woke.

He lifted his head from his desk and looked around the room. Ms. Bednard was still out of sight, dragging boxes.

He looked at his watch. It was blurry. Cole closed his eyes for a moment, then opened them and checked again. The watch was still blurry.

He looked over at Benjie, who had turned toward the other side of the room. Cole tapped him on the shoulder.

"Am I awake?" he asked.

Benjie turned toward him. "Sandwiches sing softly in the moonlight," he said. His face was the face of a raccoon.

Cole almost ruined things by screaming. He gulped down his shout. His mind yelled, *This is a dream! This is a dream! You did it!*

"Careful," Cole whispered to himself. The articles warned that you could lose your chance to stay in a lucid dream by getting too excited and waking up.

Benjie opened his raccoon mouth and pulled out a colored handkerchief.

This is it! Cole thought. He stood. *I could fly around the room.*

But that wasn't good enough. He wanted his first flight to be a memorable swoop across the sky, and not the frantic flapping of a trapped bird circling the classroom. No, he wanted it to be more than just memorable. He wanted it to be spectacular. He'd swoop under the crossbars of the football-field goalposts like a barnstorming pilot, and burst through the clouds like a superhero.

The window was open.

Cole ran to it. He leaped out. He spread his arms.

Cole fell.

His classroom was on the second floor.

A terrible thought hit Cole as he plummeted. During his research, he'd read that if you dream about falling and actually hit the ground, you'll die.

"Fly!" Cole shouted, trying desperately to take control of his dream.

Cole continued to fall.

Cole did not hit the ground.

Fortunately, there was a huge Dumpster directly below him.

Unfortunately, it was overflowing with garbage.

Fortunately, the garbage was in plastic bags, which broke his fall.

Unfortunately, his fall broke the bags.

More unfortunately, the bags contained the refuse from yesterday's lunch of sloppy joes, fish sticks, and butterscotch pudding.

Most unfortunately, the sun had beat down on the black plastic bags all of yesterday afternoon, baking the contents into a bacteria stew with a smell best left undescribed.

Cole splatted into the rotting muck without breaking any bones, or bruising anything other than his ego. He stared at his hand. It was slimed with a mix of pudding and beef, but it wasn't at all fuzzy.

By the time he'd climbed out of the Dumpster, his entire class had spilled through the door and circled the impact zone.

Ms. Bednard was simultaneously screaming at him for pulling such a stupid stunt, and asking him if he was hurt.

Cole ignored her and stared at Benjie, who no longer looked like a raccoon.

Benjie flashed him a grin and held up the rubber mask and red bandana. He mouthed the words, "Got you."

As the truth hit Cole, he touched his watch. It had been smeared with something to make the display look blurry.

"Maple syrup," Benjie said.

"I didn't get my dream," Cole said.

"I did," Benjie said. "I always wanted to pull off the perfect joke. And this was even better than I'd dreamed it would be." He laughed.

"I'll get you back," Cole said. He tried to rub the syrup off his watch face, but it remained blurry.

"Dream on," Benjie said. He laughed even louder. Then he turned away from Cole and flew off into the air, swooping under the goalpost and zooming toward the clouds.

BANGS IN YOUR EYES

Marvin was staring at his calculator when it exploded.

"Whoa!" he shouted as he leaped out of his chair and backed away from his desk. Had this been an Olympic event, he would have scored only about five points for his landing, but he did manage to remain on his feet. He looked around the bedroom, not sure what had happened. The window was closed, so nothing had come from outside. He checked the doorway, wondering whether one of his friends had somehow managed to sneak up the stairs and chuck a firecracker into the room.

There was nobody in sight. Marvin turned his attention back to the desk. Smoldering pieces of the calculator lay scattered across the surface, giving off a smell like when truckers hit the brakes too hard on a steep hill. Other pieces had shot across his bedroom. One small shard of black plastic even made it as far as his bed.

Marvin tentatively reached out and touched a metallic fragment. It was warm. That told him nothing.

The battery? . . . he thought. He'd heard of defective batteries exploding. But this was a solar calculator. It ran off room light, even in a fairly dim room. He wasn't even sure whether it had a battery until he spotted a tiny silvery disk on the floor.

He scraped the pieces off his desk into his trash can, making sure there wasn't any paper in there to catch fire. The smoldering had stopped, but he didn't want to take any chances. The can was empty. The pieces clanked against the metal bottom.

Three days later, Marvin's wristwatch exploded while he was sitting on the floor of his living room, watching TV. That hurt. But not too badly. It was a small explosion, and most of the force went outward, leaving the back plate of the watch fairly intact but blowing the face and circuitry halfway across the room. Marvin found the intact watch battery under the couch.

He looked for any connection between the watch and the calculator. *I was staring at the watch. Did I stare at the calculator?* He thought back three days, to the time of the first explosion. Yes, he'd been staring at the calculator, angry that his math teacher had given the class extra homework to punish them for talking. Actually, to punish all of them for Marvin talking.

And a moment ago, when the watch exploded, he'd been angry that he was missing the movie all his friends had gone to see. His parents told him they didn't have time to drive him to the Cineplex at the mall. His friend Todd's mom was taking all the other kids, but there wasn't room for Marvin. From what he knew, there'd been room for *everyone* else. Just no room for him. Todd never seemed to have room for Marvin these days. Marvin got more and more angry as he watched the minutes click toward the starting time of the movie.

He remembered something odd that had happened the instant before each explosion. There'd been a red glow. It wasn't strong and bright, like the ones in a traffic light or on top of a police car. It was a tint, like sunlight would make on a wall if it passed through a red piece of glass. And there'd been a hum. No—not a hum. It was clicks. But they were so close together, they seemed like one steady sound.

I wonder if I can make something else explode? That could be sort of fun. Or sort of amazing. He imagined making his math teacher's watch blow up. Or Todd's calculator, just when the nearsighted geek was squinting at it and holding it inches from his eyes. That would be perfect.

Marvin went up to his bedroom to find something he wouldn't miss. He had a small collection of old action figures in the bottom drawer of his desk. He grabbed the one he liked the least, stood it on the seat of his chair, knelt in front of it, clenched his fists, and stared.

Nothing happened, except his hands got sweaty.

Maybe it has to be electronics.

He found another watch. His aunts and uncles didn't have a lot of imagination when it came to presents.

Marvin stared at the watch for a while. It remained as unexploded as the action figure. Then he remembered that he wasn't just staring at the things that blew up. He was glaring.

He tried glaring at the watch, but that just made his face hurt. *Maybe I really have to be angry.* He figured that would make a difference. Fake anger wasn't very strong.

He thought back to the other watch. He was angry with his parents for not driving him to the movie. But he was even angrier with Todd for not giving him one of the seats in the car.

"You call yourself a friend. You stupid, nearsighted, squinting, loser, fake friend."

Marvin glared at the watch, making sure not to point it directly at his own eyes. A hum made of frantic clicks rose from his wrist, a slight red glow blossomed over the face, and the watch exploded.

"Awesome," Marvin whispered.

He grabbed the action figure, worked up a gut full of anger, and blew the toy to pieces. He realized it wasn't just electronics. He could blow up all sorts of things. He could blow up anything at all.

The full meaning of this hit him. *He'd discovered a super-power.* He was always imagining what it would be like to lift a car over his head with super strength, or to knock people off their feet with the power of his mind. But this wasn't a fantasy or a pretend power, like a kid running around with a cape or a plastic sword. This was real.

His body tingled and his mind surged like someone had replaced his blood with electricity.

"I have unbelievable power," he whispered. He could become an authentic superhero. "Fear me."

He just had to figure out the best way to use his power. "Don't be stupid with it," he said. It would be easy to start fooling around, blowing things up. There had to be a smarter way. If he made the right choices, he knew he could become rich and powerful.

I could work for the government! He could be an assassin. He pictured himself eliminating the bad guys. That was it. He could be a secret agent. Maybe, if sight was the key to his power, he could even blow things up through binoculars or a telescope. He'd be unstoppable, and uncatchable. He'd be the most feared assassin in the world.

"I need a costume," he said. "Maybe a cool mask. Or a fancy suit, like a superspy."

He crossed his room and looked at himself in the mirror. He

could just picture himself in an expensive suit, like the spies in the movies, gliding elegantly through a party at an embassy, looking for his target.

But I never get invited to parties.

The thought interrupted his fantasy. The thought also led to another, and another, as he brooded about all the times his so-called friends had left him out of parties, movies, or games.

"I hate all of you!" he shouted, glaring at the mirror. "And I'm going to make all of you suffer. I'm going to blow up everything you own." Forget the stupid spy stuff. He was going to punish the rotten losers who pretended to be his friends, but never really liked him. All the kids who left him out of everything were in for a real surprise. Maybe he'd invite them to a surprise party.

But they'd never come. They'd promise to come, lying right to his face. And then, they'd stand him up, and laugh about it behind his back. That thought fueled his rage. There'd be no party. He'd have to hunt them down one by one.

"You're all doomed!" he shouted, glaring into the mirror.

He was so angry, he didn't even notice the ticking at first. But he definitely saw the red tinge that washed over his face.

"No!" Marvin screamed as he realized what he'd triggered.

The faceplate of the calculator . . . the face of the watch . . . the face of the action figure. His anger, his power, worked on faces as he glared at them.

Before Marvin could say anything more, his head exploded. It made a much larger mess than the watch had.

THE TALK

A bunch of different reactions ran through the class when the announcement was made. Behind me, I could hear Kenny Harcourt snickering. On my right, I saw Mary Beth Adderly whisper something to Kara Chen. Kara blushed. On my left, Tyler Horvath looked up at the speaker with no expression. Next to Tyler, Eddie Moldour was wearing a smug grin.

I listened as the announcement was repeated. "All sixth-grade girls please report to the auditorium," Principal Sestwick said.

We knew what that meant. It was time for *The Talk*. Even though the guys were left out, it was no big secret to us what would happen. They'd get the girls together and explain stuff about puberty and growing up. It was also no big deal—for guys. We had it simple and easy.

"All sixth-grade boys please report to the gym," Principal Sestwick added.

"Great," I said, turning around toward Bobby Mussleman. "Maybe we'll get to play dodgeball while they talk to the girls."

"That sounds good," Bobby said. "Wouldn't be fair if they made us sit here and work."

We got up and headed to the gym, while our teacher, Mr. Mercante, made a few halfhearted attempts to keep us from running, pushing, or talking too loudly. At the gym doors, we merged with the boys from the other three sixth-grade classes.

I expected to see our gym teacher waiting for us. Instead, Principal Sestwick came in and went over to a microphone that had been set up at one end of the gym.

"Sit down, boys," he said.

I grabbed a spot on the floor, next to Eddy. "What's up?" I asked.

"No idea," he said.

"In the next few years," the principal said, "you'll begin to notice some changes."

Next to me, Eddy squinted at his hand, then, in a fake scream, he whispered, "I've got hair on my knuckles. Oh no, save me! I'm changing!"

I choked down the laugh that was threatening to explode out of my mouth. It was a good thing I wasn't drinking milk—the spray would have shot three or four feet from my nose. "Cut it out," I managed to say when I'd gotten back in control.

The principal was still talking, even though Eddy and I weren't the only ones who were horsing around. "In the beginning, some of this might frighten or confuse you," he said, "but please keep in mind that everything that happens is perfectly natural."

He paused and looked across the crowd, then went on with The Talk. "The first signs might be very small. One day, you'll find yourself reading the newspaper. And not just sports and comics, but also the news."

"What's he talking about?" I asked Eddy.

"No idea," Eddy said.

"I read the paper," Tyler said.

Someone behind him said, "Who cares?" and smacked him on the head.

"You'll find yourself keeping track of your money," Principal Sestwick said. "You might even make out a budget. Eventually, you'll consider opening a checking account as a first step toward establishing credit."

Principal Sestwick took a deep breath, then went on. "As these changes occur, you'll even find yourself looking at insurance policies, as well as . . ."

He kept on talking. I was almost too shocked to listen. Around us, I could see kids staring at the principal with amazement. The stuff he was talking about . . .

"These are things our parents do," I said aloud as the realization struck me. "He's saying we're going to do them, too!"

"Not me," Eddie said. "I'm never doing any of that. No way."

A wave of revulsion rippled through me. "But our parents—"

"Shut up." Eddie cut me off. "Don't talk about it."

I had to agree with him. *Not me,* I thought. *Never.*

A few minutes later, The Talk was over. We all got up, rising like zombies, stiff and stunned and dazed. We'd been pelted with terms like *annuities, compound interest, and comprehensive coverage.* On the way back to class, we ran into the girls. They were mostly looking pretty giggly. A few of them looked embarrassed but, all in all, they looked a lot better than the boys around me.

Kara caught my eye. She was more mature than the other girls, and she didn't seem embarrassed to be coming back from the girl's version of The Talk.

"What did you boys do?" she asked.

"Dodgeball," I said before I even had a chance to think.

"Lucky you," Kara said.

"Yeah. Lucky us."

SAME BIRD

Isabel and Avi were hiking in the woods with their parents. Isabel and Avi's parents thought hiking was a wonderful family activity. Isabel and Avi thought otherwise, but they didn't dislike the great outdoors enough to complain about the situation. They were quite familiar with the phrase, "Pick your battles," and quite expert at applying that wisdom.

Avi knew that if he complained about the hike, his parents would be less likely to pay attention to him when he tried to convince them to switch to a better Internet service provider.

Isabel knew that if she complained about the hike, she'd have a harder time arguing with her parents for a later curfew when she went out with her friends on Saturday nights.

So they suffered, moderately, in a silence which they dotted with quiet sighs and rolling eyes. Sure, nature was grand and beautiful and majestic. But it was also highly repetitive. It might be true that no two snowflakes were alike. But it was also true that pretty much every snowflake was really really really similar to every other snowflake when viewed without the aid of a microscope or magnifying glass.

At least it wasn't snowing. That wasn't a big surprise, since the family was hiking a trail in southern California. Adding to the irony, Avi and Isabel's parents owned a flower shop, which meant they were doing a very bad job of escaping from work by heading for the great outdoors.

"What's that?" Avi asked as he spotted something that was not green or brown at the edge of the endless brown trail lined with an endless expanse of green plants and brown-limbed trees.

"A feather?" Isabel suggested.

Avi glanced ahead, to make sure his parents weren't watching. His mom seemed to think that certain items carried enough germs to instantly sicken, cripple, or kill the healthiest kid. Bird feathers were very close to the top of that list, bested only by rat corpses, anything festering in a public trash can, and Stinky Minkowitz, their one neighbor who seemed clueless about basic hygiene and sanitation.

His mom was talking with his dad about adult stuff involving taxes. Avi picked up the feather. It was large and red, with streaks of silver. No, not silver. As Avi looked closer, he decided the color was more like steel than silver. He swiped the feather in the direction of his sister, to see if she shared their mother's aversion. She didn't.

"Peacock?" Avi guessed, naming the only large bird he could think of that had colorful feathers.

"In the woods?" Isabel asked, giving her voice the medium-high-level tone of mockery she reserved for absurd questions that came from people she was, at times, somewhat fond of.

"Good point." Avi decided he didn't need to know immediately, or maybe even ever at all, what kind of bird the feather came from.

"What's that?" Isabel said, a short while later. She bent and plucked something from the middle of a bush.

Avi looked at the feather his sister held. "Same bird," he said.

"Yeah," Isabel said. "Same bird." On this, they could agree.

They found five more feathers in the next hundred yards. Each time, Avi said, "Same bird."

Each time, Isabel nodded, and said, "Same bird."

Ahead of them, their parents hiked, talked, and cast the occasional glance back to make sure they hadn't lost the rest of their family.

Soon after that, Avi found an entire wing.

It took him a moment to gather his wits and say, "Same bird." It was a large wing. But the red and steel feathers left no doubt.

"Let me see." Isabel took the wing and examined it. The bit of flesh and bone she could see at the severed end also had a metallic shimmer. "Yeah, same bird."

They found a foot and a beak before they found the second wing.

Eventually, guided by their basic knowledge of bird anatomy, gained mostly from the rotisserie chickens their parents bought when neither of them felt like cooking dinner, Avi and Isabel were fairly certain they'd found an entire bird. That was good since they'd reached the limits of their carrying capacity. Their arms were loaded, and both of them kept dropping pieces. In its current disassembled condition, the bird remained unidentifiable by either of the kids.

"Let's see if we can put it together," Avi said.

"You can't put it together," Isabel said. "That's a really stupid suggestion."

Avi replied with a glare. He wasn't stupid, and his sister knew it.

"Sorry," she said. She took a wing and pressed it against the side of the bird body.

Click.

The wing snapped into place as if the pieces were magnetized.

"Told you," Avi said.

He handed Isabel the second wing. She put it on the other side of the body.

They knelt, spread the remaining pieces in front of them, and began reassembling the bird.

"Hey, what are you kids doing?" their dad called.

"Stop dawdling," their mom called.

"Hurry," Avi whispered, turning his back to his parents. There weren't a lot of pieces left. He wasn't sure what he and Isabel were going to do with the bird once it was assembled, but he knew he'd have a better chance of doing what he wanted with it if they got the whole thing together before their parents realized what it was.

Ignoring the crunch of two pairs of hiking boots coming toward them on the trail, Avi and Isabel rushed to finish assembling the bird. Never, since the days of Hansel and Gretel, had a brother and sister exhibited such dazzling teamwork in the middle of the woods. A moment later, Avi held up the last piece, which happened to be the first feather he'd found. He scanned the bird to see where the feather belonged. The bird stood there, tall and majestic, looking like a mix between a stork and pterodactyl.

"There," Isabel said, pointing to a spot on the left side, above the wing.

"Got it," Avi said, placing the feather where it belonged. He rose from his knees and took a step back to admire the finished bird. Assembled, it was at least three feet tall.

"Cool," Avi said.

"Awesome," Isabel said.

"What are you kids doing?" their father said.

"Is that a bird?" their mother said.

"Rawwwkk," the bird said.

It opened its eyes just as Avi and Isabel's parents reached them.

Then it attacked.

There were screams and cries, but no flying feathers. The bird remained assembled. The happy hiking family did not. The great outdoors had failed to bring them together.

The next day, a sparrow that, like all sparrows, lacked a name, landed on the trail, along with his nameless friend.

"What's that?" the sparrow asked, aiming his beak in the direction of a not-soil-brown or leaf-green object lying in the middle of the trail, like a solitary mushroom.

"Looks like a toe," his friend said, after examining the object.

They hopped farther along the trail.

"There's another one," his friend said.

The sparrow went closer and studied the toe. "Same kid?" he asked.

"Yeah," his friend said. "Same kid."

HAUNTING YOUR THOUGHTS

I wish I'd figured it out sooner. I wish I'd seen the truth right after we'd moved in, or maybe even before then. That could have saved me. It could have saved all of us. But everything seemed fine at first. I guess that's part of how it works. It needed to keep us unaware of what was happening for long enough to create the real horror.

"Like it, Ruthie?" Mom asked, the first time I went inside.

I shrugged and let out something along the lines of "Uh-huh." I mean, it was a house. Big deal. We'd left one house and were moving to another. This one was older. But I didn't connect the tiny chill that ran across my scalp when I walked through the door with anything dangerous. I hardly noticed it.

"I like it!" my little brother, Yantzy, shouted. He dashed toward the stairs that led up to the bedrooms on the second floor, then looked back and asked, "There aren't any ants, are there?"

"It's winter," Mom said. "Of course there aren't any ants."

I mouthed the words, "Giant ants," and wriggled my fingers over my head like bug antennas.

I guess Mom could tell Yantzy was staring at me, because she spun around fast enough to catch me in the act. "Stop scaring your brother," she said.

"He's not scared," I said. "He's tough." That was actually true, for the most part. Yantzy didn't scare easily. Except when it came to ants. But, as Mom had already pointed out to him, it was winter. And winter in Connecticut wasn't an ant-friendly time or place.

Mom has her own issues. Everything in her world has to be lined up perfectly before she can relax. And I do mean *perfectly*. Right after we moved in, she and Dad spent two whole days putting up pictures, curtains, and shelves. Dad has this laser level, so he could straighten picture frames to one-hundred-billionth of an inch, or something ridiculous like that, to keep Mom happy.

I stayed out of their way. That wasn't hard. I had my own room, which I liked—at first.

Then, about a week or so after we moved in, I started to hear the scratching sound. I thought it was rats. That actually wouldn't bother me. I like rodents. But the sound didn't come from close to the floor. It was about the same height as my chest. Heart-high. Yeah. That's what it was.

I pictured some sort of rotting monster, with long, filthy claws, feeling its way around the house, staying behind the walls. I know that's silly. Fearing monsters behind walls was just like Yantzy fearing ants in winter. This was even sillier than that, I guess. There really are ants. Maybe not in the winter, but they're still real. There aren't any rotting monsters with filthy claws, winter or summer.

The next day, I heard a scream while I was eating breakfast. It was Mom. Okay—not a real scream, like you'd hear in a horror movie. It was more like a cry of frustration. I tracked the sound to the living room. Mom was staring at the wall above the fireplace. There were four framed photos there. At first, I couldn't even tell what she was bothered about. Then, I noticed that the photo on the right was just a little bit crooked.

Mom told me to get the ladder from the basement. That's not my favorite place, but you don't argue with a screamer. And the ladder is really light, so I didn't have any trouble carrying it up the steps. But Mom wouldn't let me straighten the picture. She made Dad come do it, with his laser level.

As Dad tottered up there on the ladder, straightening the photo, he said, "There's a draft."

"Don't worry about it," Mom said.

But Dad was worried. Drafts were his thing. He hated the fuel bill. He hated wasted energy. Wherever we'd lived, he was always hunting around for drafts. Twelve times a year, when the fuel bill came in the mail, he got especially angry.

The problem is, the picture didn't stay straight for long, no matter what Dad did to try to keep it from shifting. None of the pictures behaved. It was like someone was sneaking around the house, tilting things just slightly. And in every room, at random times, there'd be these strange drafts floating through the air, chilling us and making the heater kick in. Dad was never able to find a source for them.

Then, about a month after we moved in, Yantzy came down from his room, screaming, "Ants! Lots of ants!"

"I got this," I said, before my parents could spring from the couch, where they were watching a movie. I went up to Yantzy's room, dragging him along so he could point out where he saw the ants.

He tugged against my grip and tried to break free, but I was a lot stronger. "Show me," I said.

"There." He pointed toward his dresser. "Under it."

I walked over and leaned down. I couldn't see anything in the inch or two between the bottom drawer and the floor. I went around to the side, to look from there. But as I leaned against the wall, I heard a slashing scratch, like something was trying to rip my ear off. I could picture claws shredding the wall on the other side, trying to get through and attack me.

"No!" I shouted and backed away. My heart was hammering like it was planning to leave the room immediately, whether or not I joined it. I forced myself to calm down.

"There aren't any ants," I said. "It's winter."

Yantzy shook his head and fled the room. I peeked under the dresser again. I still didn't see anything. But I didn't want to hang out in there, near that wall.

From then on, I stayed away from the house as much as I could. I'd go to the library or to a friend's house. Or even the park. But I had to come home to go to sleep. And that's when the scratching was the worst.

Finally, about six weeks after we'd moved in, I knew I had to do something. "We should look for another house," I said when we sat down to dinner.

Mom and Dad stared at me, but they didn't say anything. Yantzy, on the other hand, was immediately and loudly in favor of a move.

After dinner, I followed Dad into the living room. Just as we got there, I saw a painting on the wall near the top of the stairs tilt. Right before my eyes, it tilted.

There was no possible cause. I hadn't felt any vibration, like when a heavy truck drives down the road. I hadn't heard the creak and crack that comes when the wind hits a house with a strong gust. The paintings on either side of the tilted one remained unmoved.

Mom came in just after that. She spotted the misaligned painting instantly. "Get the level," she told Dad.

He sighed and headed to the garage for his tool kit. After he returned, I saw the curtains flutter on the wall opposite the painting. A cold draft blew in, even though the window was closed. Just then, Yantzy screamed.

This time, as he fled from his room and ran down the stairs, I saw something dark flowing after him across the white carpet, like gallons of spilled ink.

Ants. Lots of them.

I'm not a genius, but sometimes I can think my way through complicated problems, or put together a theory based on a series of observations. This was one of those times.

Everyone in my family was afraid of something. Mom feared disorder and irregularity. Dad feared waste. Yantzy feared ants. The house kept hitting them with what they feared the most.

It wasn't their imagination. Each fear was real. I saw the ants. I felt the breeze that rippled the curtains. I saw the picture tilt.

But those were all mild fears. Mine wasn't.

I was afraid of monsters. I didn't fear just the noises I heard. I feared the things that made the noise, those dark, misshapen creatures that hid behind walls and lurked within shadows. I'd started hearing the sounds those creatures made soon after we moved to this house.

That meant . . .

I tried not to follow the thought to the inevitable conclusion, but there was no escape from it. Like the ants, the tilted pictures, and the drafts, the monsters had to be real, too.

I spun around, wondering which wall hid them. I didn't have to wonder for long.

It was all the walls.

The monsters burst into the room from all around us.

Suddenly, I wasn't alone in my fear. As the rotted corpselike creatures with their broken teeth and jagged nails swarmed at us, we all screamed.

Fear gave way to pain. Pain gave way to darkness.

I hoped the next owners of the house had safer fears.

DIFFERNET EXPLORER

Hector typed baldly. No, wait. That's not right. Hector typed badly. This was not a symptom of poor spelling ability or an inadequate education. The cause was simple and obvious; he was careless and somewhat lacking in fine motor skills. He'd never make a good surgeon, or knitter. Fortunately, he'd never imagined himself chasing either of those pursuits, so he wasn't doomed to a lifetime of disappointment, asymmetrical sweaters, or malpractice suits.

Hector was grateful for spell-checkers. But when he was writing reports for school, he sometimes typed things so badly that even the spell-checker didn't have a clue what word he had in mind. But we're not here to discuss the times he completely missed the majority of letters in a word, clumsily striking adjacent keys, to produce something like *dtrimf* for *string*, or struck two letters by mistake, turning *special* into *specvialk*.

It was one of Hector's subtler mistakes that concerns us today. His school, having generated an excess of funds by way of eliminating all art and music classes, invested in an extraordinarily expensive suite of software that was marketed to administrators as the perfect writing environment for students. Among its many features was a complex system of hypertext. Basically, as a student wrote words, the software relentlessly scoured the vast depths of the Internet to identify and offer supporting material, research, definitions, and an endless stream of other distractions that was so dense it made writing far more difficult than it needed to be.

As an example of the problem, a student writing about frogs of the Amazonian rain forest would, upon typing the word "frog," be offered links to scientific articles about frogs, audio files of frog sounds, images of frogs, and perhaps even the ancient play by Aristophanes, named *The Frogs*.

With great power comes great opportunities for disaster. But we are getting ahead of the story. As noted, Hector's mistake was subtle. It was a mistake he'd made many times before, but never in a hypertext environment.

While working on an essay about diversity, instead of typing *different*, Hector typed *differnet*. Most links that showed up in response to properly spelled words appeared almost immediately. This one, responding to a minor typographical error, took slightly longer than half a second, which to computers must seem like eons, epochs, or perhaps even *I thought you were never coming back*. To the human eye, specifically Hector's eye, conditioned to immediate underscoring and highlighting, this delay was like a flashbulb to the retina.

"Differnet," he said, absorbing his mistake. He hovered his cursor over the word, and checked the link text. *Enter the Differnet*.

"Sure," Hector said. He was not just careless and clumsy. He was also lazy. Any distraction from the task at hand was welcome. He clicked himself into the *Differnet*.

It looked a lot like the Internet. Icons floated on the screen, offering video clips and news stories. Hector saw one with a man standing at the top of a skyscraper. Above the image, in the typically overexaggerated language of the Internet, the caption read: *This BASE-jumping video will take your breath away!*

"Cool," Hector said, clicking the image.

The video played. A man stood at the edge of the rooftop on a skyscraper that towered above everything else in sight. The screen was split, with one view coming from a camera on the roof, and the other from a camera in the man's helmet.

The man jumped. The plunge was spectacular—especially with the split-screen images. When the man was roughly halfway down, Hector realized he needed air. His lungs were crying out for him to take a breath.

He inhaled.

Or tried to.

He couldn't breathe. As promised, the Differnet video had taken his breath away. After a moment of panic, Hector killed the video.

"Phew," he said on his first exhalation, which followed his deep and greedy inhalation the instant his breath was returned to him. "That was different."

He saw another video, this time involving stunt jets, which promised to *make your jaw drop.*

Being a very slow learner, Hector clicked the image. His jaw did drop. Not to the floor, fortunately, or off his face. It just dropped to the point where anyone seeing his face would have no doubt that he was startled.

This is weird, Hector thought as the video ended and his mandible ascended. He scrolled among the vast and various offerings on the Differnet.

What this toddler does will make you laugh so hard, you'll wet your pants!

"No thanks," Hector said.

When you see the hilarious prank these students pull on their classmate, milk will shoot out of your nose.

"Yeah, right," Hector said. He clicked PLAY.

The stunt was hilarious.

Milk shot out of his nose.

Fortunately, he felt it coming and turned his head aside, so he didn't drench his keyboard.

He bypassed offers to roll on the floor, laugh a certain part of his body off, scream with delight, or gasp in amazement. Then, he saw a video of his favorite thing of all, a clip of skateboarding stunts.

Hector, who was in the habit of clicking on anything even marginally interesting without giving his actions too much thought, clicked PLAY while he was reading the caption: *This clip of two dudes jumping over moving cars on their skateboards will absolutely slay you.*

On-screen, the two dudes jumped. Offscreen, Hector was slain. Absolutely.

Hector's tragic death will literally make you cry oceans of tears. It will blow your mind. It will change your life forever. It will . . . Wait. No. It probably won't. Never mind.

HEALED

Nobody would tell me what was wrong with me. I knew I was sick. My body ached like I'd been tackled by fifteen kids. Fifteen times. My head felt fuzzy. I didn't have any energy. I could barely get out of bed. I didn't even *want* to get out of bed. Mom took me to one doctor after another. They spewed big words at her, but not anything that I could figure out how to spell well enough so I could look it up on the Internet. No two of the doctors seemed to think I had the same thing.

Finally, Mom heard about Dr. Spavisker. "They call him the Miracle Man," she told Dad. Her voice dropped lower when she spoke the last two words, as if they were some sort of sacred spell. She held up a magazine that had an article about him.

"I hope they're right," Dad said.

"What's wrong with me?" I asked, for the thousandth time.

"Oh, nothing, sweetie," Mom said, for the thousandth time. But she looked away when I tried to watch her face and find a clue in her eyes to the truth.

Dr. Spavisker had a clinic in Arizona, about 150 miles away from where we lived. My parents took me there the next day. It was a long drive, but I napped for most of it, so I didn't really notice the time passing.

They put me in a room with another kid. He looked really sick, like he could die at any moment. That scared me. I realized that was what I must look like. I mean, I saw myself in the mirror every day, but I don't think anyone really sees himself when he looks in a mirror. If something changes slowly, you might not even notice it at all. I checked around the room for a mirror, but didn't see one. I guess that was probably a good thing.

But I really wanted to find out if I looked as bad as the kid in the other bed. So I asked if I could use the bathroom.

"Of course, Donovan," Mom said. "This is your room now. Until you get better."

I went into the bathroom, closed the door, and tried to really see my face. I almost wish I hadn't. My goldfish died last year. Its eyes looked just like mine. Flat. Lifeless. I didn't want to stare at myself anymore. I went back to the room.

Dr. Spavisker had joined my parents. He was an old guy, with white hair on the sides of his head and thick glasses. "Ah, Donovan," he said, holding out his hand, "I'm so glad you're here. Don't you worry. I'll see that your parents get back the son they thought they lost, as good as new. Better than new!"

He gave my shoulder a squeeze, then turned to my dad. "We'll start running our tests immediately. I'll keep the two of you informed at every step."

Mom and Dad said good-bye, then headed off. Instead of saying anything to me, Dr. Spavisker went to the window and looked out. I guess he was watching them leave. They'd wanted to stay in a hotel nearby, so they could visit me, but they'd been told it was better to go home and wait. I could hear a car pulling away. After the sound faded, the doctor stepped back from the window and said, "Let's get started."

I glanced down at my right arm. "Are you going to be taking a lot of blood?" I'd been stuck so many times, I was surprised I had any blood left.

"No, I don't need blood samples." He reached into his shirt pocket and pulled out some sort of tube. He uncapped the tube and removed a stick. I saw it had a cotton swab at the end.

"Open wide," he said.

I opened my mouth. I was so used to doing whatever the doctors told me, I would pretty much follow any order. Open wide, breathe in, spit out, swallow, look at the ceiling, and so on. He rubbed the swab against the inside of my cheek, then put it back in the tube and slipped it into his pocket.

"That's it?" I asked.

"That's it. All of our work is based on very sophisticated DNA testing and analysis." He pointed to the bed. "Get comfortable. It will be at least a week or two before we have any results."

A week or two? I looked for some way to kill a bit of time. My roommate was sleeping. There was a bookcase next to my bed with a collection of paperbacks. There was also an old computer with some games. "Internet?" I asked.

"Sorry. We're too far from the city, and nobody is willing to run cable out here. There aren't any cell towers, and the mountains block the satellite signals. But most of our patients discover they don't really miss it after a day or two. We get a newspaper, so you can keep up with the world. And several magazines."

"Well, that's great," I muttered. I suspected I had a good chance of dying of boredom before the doctor figured out anything. I grabbed a book and plopped down on the bed.

The time did pass pretty painlessly, mostly because I slept a lot. The other kid, Bradley, didn't talk much. We said "Hi" to each other at one point. I might have said "Cool" when we saw an Apache helicopter fly past.

They always locked our door at night. I thought that was kind of weird. Then, on my fourth or fifth night, the guy who locks the doors got distracted and forgot to close ours.

I really didn't think there was anything to see. But I was bored. Night and day were all the same. I slept, I woke, I slept some more. So it wasn't surprising that I woke up in the middle of the night. I slipped out through the doorway, into the corridor.

I found there were five other rooms on the floor, each with two kids. There was one floor above me, and one below. I checked both. There were five more rooms above, with kids. There were offices and labs on the first floor. I also found a door to a basement.

It was creepy going down there, but I'd been sick for so long, I really didn't have enough energy for fear. At least, not until I got down there and saw the vats.

Yeah, vats.

They were big ones, twice the size of a bathtub, made of thick, clear glass, and filled with a pale-green liquid. They took up the whole basement.

Kids floated in them.

Not just any kids.

I saw myself. And I saw my roommate.

He was full size. I was smaller, though it was hard to tell how much. The glass and the liquid distorted the images. My fingers and toes didn't seem fully formed. But I could recognize my face.

I got out of there and hurried back to the room.

Clones . . . I thought. Dr. Spavisker wasn't healing anyone. He was growing clones. Growing them really quickly, somehow.

And then what?

He couldn't just hand a clone over to some parents and say, "Here's your kid, as good as new." Not without doing something about the clone's mind.

Maybe he transplanted the brain.

I felt the skin of my skull shiver at that thought. Were brain transplants even possible?

All of a sudden, I really missed the Internet.

But forget brain transplants—cloning itself wasn't possible, as far as I knew. Not for a person. Definitely not for a person you could grow in a week or two. But there they'd been, right in front of me. Maybe a brain transplant was possible, too.

Or maybe Dr. Spavisker told the parents that the cure had caused brain damage. *Here's your son. Sorry he doesn't remember much. But at least he's healthy.*

I slipped back to my room and sat in my bed, waiting for the sun to rise and hoping I'd wake up from this nightmare.

But morning came, and I had to face the truth that the vats hadn't been a dream. I looked over at Bradley. Based on the development of his clone, he'd be *cured* before me. I had to find out if he stayed the same.

"Good morning," I said when he woke up.

"Morning, Donovan," he said.

"I hate that name," I said, using the lie I'd invented during the night. "My friends call me Chuck, because I used to throw up a lot." I figured that would be easy to remember. "It started out as 'Upchuck,' but got shortened to just plain old 'Chuck.'"

"Morning, Chuck," he said. "What's up?" He gave me a weak smile to show he was making a joke.

For the next two days, I talked to him often enough to reinforce that name. It was now in his mind—part of the data in his brain. To him, I was Chuck. If I managed to see him after he was *cured*, I'd be able to test his memory. And if his memory was intact, I could stop worrying and let my brain, or my memories, or whatever, be put in a healthy body.

I hoped it happened soon. I was getting weaker every day. On the third day after I'd become "Chuck," I could hardly get out of bed. Bradley was even worse.

The next morning, they wheeled him out. Late that night, they brought him back in. He was asleep, or unconscious, but even so, I could tell he was healthier. His face wasn't that of a dying kid. His head was bandaged. I guess maybe, just maybe, they'd taken Bradley's brain from his sick body and put it in his clone's healthy body.

Bradley didn't wake until late the next morning. Right when he started to stir, my parents came into my room.

"We've found a better place for you," my mom said. "A doctor who can fix you right away."

"This is taking too long," my dad said. "We don't think we can trust Dr. Spavisker. There's something creepy about this place."

On the next bed, Bradley opened his eyes. He sat up like a kid who did fifty pushups and a hundred jumping jacks before breakfast. He looked like he could run a marathon.

"Bradley," I said. "How do you feel?"

"Great," he said.

"See," I told my parents. "They fixed him. They'll fix me next."

"They'll fix you right up, Chuck," Bradley said. He laughed.

"Chuck?" Dad said. He and Mom exchanged looks. "Something must have happened to that poor boy's brain. Why is he calling Donovan 'Chuck'?"

"Because Chuck throws up all the time," Bradley said. He let out another laugh.

"Let's get you out of here," Mom said. She ran to the closet where my clothes were. "There's no time to waste."

"But . . ." I tried to argue. I tried to explain that Dr. Spavisker could fix me. I was too weak to put together more than a couple words. They took me away. We're driving to a new place. I hope that doctor can make clones fast. Real fast.

STUNT YOUR GROWTH

Ricky was running through the mall at top speed when the mall cop made a grab for him.

"No running," the mall cop shouted.

No contest, Ricky thought. He dodged, twisted, stutter-stepped, and dashed away from the clutching hands, laughing. He put on an extra burst of speed, just to drive home the reality that he was uncatchable, then slowed his pace once he no longer heard the gasping, wheezing sounds of pursuit or the pathetic slap of clumsy footfalls against the mall's plastic fake wood floor.

He turned a corner by the pretzel shop and dropped down to a regular walk, scanning the windows of the sneaker store and pizza place as he headed for the exit.

"Hey, kid . . ."

Ricky nearly jumped out of his skin when he felt the tap on his shoulder. He looked back, ready to harness more energy and make a dash for the exit. But it wasn't a mall cop. It was a guy in a flashy Hawaiian shirt, with heavy gold chains around his neck, glittery rings on every single finger, and a pair of the latest sunglasses perched on his face.

"What?" Ricky asked. He didn't know much about jewelry, but the glittery stuff the guy had on looked pretty expensive, and the sunglasses were definitely the type that cost a fortune.

"Here." The man handed Ricky a business card.

Ricky read the name, and then the title. Buster Grogan, Stunt Coordinator. He spoke the second part. "Stunt coordinator?"

The man nodded. "I'm in charge of stunts for movies. We're shooting one just outside of town. It's an action flick. I need a kid who can run and dodge, like you did back there. You're the perfect height and weight for the job."

"I'd be in a movie?" Ricky asked.

"For sure. And you'd get paid."

"How much?" Ricky asked.

The man told him. Ricky whistled. He rarely whistled, but it was a lot of money. A whole lot of money. Enough for a fistful of sunglasses. "What do I have to do?"

"Run."

"I can do that," Ricky said.

"Do you know the river canyon, out past the old Parker ranch?" the man asked.

"Sure do," Ricky said.

"Be there tomorrow morning at 7:15. Wear blue jeans."

Ricky thought of last fall, when he'd gone out for football. "Do I need permission from my parents?"

"No point bothering them," the man said. "Parents don't understand much about this sort of thing. And they tend to be overprotective." He gave Ricky a wink and walked off.

The next morning, Ricky slipped out after breakfast and

rode his bike to the river canyon. *Be careful,* he told himself. *It could be some sort of trick.* He planned to approach the area cautiously, and leave lots of room to turn around and dash off if he saw anything that made him nervous. But as he got close, his heart sped up in a good way. He saw trucks, trailers, cameras, and lots of people. There was no doubt a movie was being shot.

When Ricky reached the edge of the set, Buster Grogan waved at him and walked over. "Hey, right on time. You ready?"

"Yeah. Sure. I think so." Ricky still had no real idea what he was supposed to do. He knew stunt people did dangerous things. That was fine. He loved danger. He figured he'd find out the details soon enough.

"Here, put this on." The man handed him a green zip-up jacket and a red ball cap. He led Ricky to the edge of the canyon, then pointed toward a spot about a quarter of the way down the face of the cliff, where a woman was placing a small red cone on a ledge. "See that?" he asked.

"Yeah."

"That's your starting point," Buster Grogan said.

"So the star ran the first part for the camera?" Ricky asked. He wanted to show that he knew how this worked. The star would get filmed doing the safe stuff, before the slope got too steep. Then the stunt person—the stunt kid, in this case— would take over for the dangerous part.

"Yup. We have the first part on film," Buster Grogan said.

Ricky was sorry he'd missed seeing that. Far off, way below them, he spotted another kid, wearing jeans, a green jacket, and a red hat, limping away from the bottom of the canyon. "Who's that?" he asked.

"That—oh, he's just a stand-in for the star. We use him to

make sure everything is in focus and the lighting is right. So, are you ready to thrill the crowds?"

"Absolutely." Ricky made his way down the slope to the cone.

The woman was standing to the side of the ledge now, out of camera range. She pointed at the cone, then held out her hand. "Toss it here."

Ricky tossed the cone to her, then waited. He knew what was coming next.

"Action!" someone cried.

Here I go! Ricky thought. He started to race down the cliff. His enthusiasm drowned out the small voice in his brain that yelled about the danger of sprinting along a steeply slanted surface. He only traveled several steps before he lost his balance.

He stumbled, staggered, skittered, and clambered, making a heroic effort to remain on his feet. He managed to do that until the midpoint of the drop, when he made a swipe at a small scrub tree that jutted from a crack in a boulder. He missed, totally lost his balance, and fell. He rolled, bounced, tumbled, plummeted, and slid the rest of the way down.

Numb, stunned, and slowly realizing he was covered with small and large cuts and bumps, Ricky staggered to his feet.

There was a guy waiting there. "I don't think I can do that again," Ricky said.

"No worries," the man said. "We figured it would take five or six kids for a complete shot. But you did so well, we might only need four." He held out a hand to lead Ricky down the path toward a car. "Let's pick up your bike. Then, I'll get you home. What's your address?"

Still too dazed to make sense of everything, Ricky looked

toward the top of the canyon, where he could vaguely hear Buster Grogan greeting a kid who had just arrived.

"Hey—7:30. Right on time. Let's get you started." He held out a jacket and hat. "Here—put this on."

Halfway down the cliff, a woman was setting the cone up, right at the spot by the small tree where Ricky had lost his footing and made the uncinematic transition from action hero to accident victim. He realized he was only one in a series of stunt kids that Buster Grogan had hired.

As Ricky got into the car, he winced in pain. But then he smiled. He was going to be in a movie. How awesome was that?

URBAN GIRL

The flowers are nice, even if I don't get to keep them for very long. The dress is pretty, but no matter how beautiful it might be, it's always the same blue, cotton, knee-length dress, with the same two pockets, and the same frills at the cuffs. A girl likes variety in her wardrobe. I guess I'd like variety in any part of my life. And I guess "life" isn't exactly right.

There's a lot of variety in who comes by, at least. It might be a car, or a van, or even a truck. But it won't be a really big truck, since they aren't supposed to be on this road. The driver can be alone, or have a passenger. In that case, I get in the backseat. It doesn't matter to me. It's not a long ride.

Some things have changed a lot over the years. Cars have changed. So have people. Long ago, the driver would just lean over to roll down the passenger-side window, cranking it by hand, and ask, "Are you lost, little girl?"

I'd lift the bouquet and say, "I picked these for my mom. I was walking home. But I got tired."

The driver would say, "Hop in."

And I would.

But people are a bit more careful these days. I understand that. Sometimes, they'll have the radio on, and I'll hear news stories. So I know what's happening in the world. Or they'll give me a lecture about how dangerous it is to be walking alone along a lonely country road after dark. Especially a road that runs right along the train tracks.

If you've ever swapped scary stories at a campout or a sleepover, you probably know how the rest of it goes. They bring me home. I ask them to make sure my mom isn't angry.

So they get out of the car and walk up the porch.

They knock on the door.

When they mention me, my mom looks shocked and tells them I've been dead for years. Hit by a train while picking flowers. They run to the car. But I'm gone. There's nothing left except for the flowers. They're on the seat.

I guess I'd feel bad if my real, living mom had to go through this. But it's not my real mom answering the door. It's not even a real person. I can see that. The people who pick me up can't.

I guess I serve some kind of purpose. I have to believe that. Otherwise, it would be unbearable to go through this every night. But don't ask me what that purpose is. I don't know.

As I said, nothing much ever really changes.

Until tonight.

It was an old car, and a young driver. That's not an unusual combination. But the car was very old, and the driver was very young.

"Lost?" he asked.

I said what I always say, telling him about picking flowers and getting tired.

"Hop in," he said.

"Are you old enough to drive?" I asked. Not that it mattered.

He was the one who stopped. I'd get in the car no matter what. That's how it worked.

He laughed. "Almost. Well, sort of . . ."

I liked the way he laughed. That was the best part of this. I got to meet all kinds of people. "What are you doing out here?" I asked as I took a seat.

"It's my mom's birthday. I got her a present." He pointed to the backseat, where there was a rabbit in a cage.

"Well, that's different," I said. My head lurched as he pulled back onto the road.

"Sorry," he said. Then he nodded. "She loves animals."

We were halfway to where I had lived when he pointed to his left and said, "That's my house. I'll take you home, and then come back. She'll never know I borrowed her car."

"I hope she likes the bunny," I said.

"She will." He glanced over his shoulder, again.

"Look out!" I screamed. He'd turned the wheel when he looked back. We were heading off the road. He swung the car hard in the other direction. He didn't seem to know how to steer very well. Tires screamed. So did I. We skidded. Then, we were rolling.

And then we weren't.

We stopped hard, with a loud crash. I wasn't hurt. I can't get hurt. He looked shaken up.

"My leg . . ." he gasped.

I looked down, then looked away.

"Call for help," he said.

I didn't have a phone. I had to go to his house. That was the closest place. "I'll be right back, with help," I said. I forced the door open. As I walked toward the road, something white caught my eye.

143

The rabbit cage had been flung from the car. I picked it up. The rabbit looked stunned, but otherwise okay.

I reached the house and knocked on the door. As soon as the woman opened it, I said, "There's been an accident. . . . Your son . . ."

And I stopped cold. The rest of the words froze in my throat. I didn't know the woman. I'd never seen her before. But I knew her expression. That look of fear and confusion, mixed with the slightest pinch of hope.

I saw that look every night when whoever was chosen to drive me home walked up my porch, knocked on my door, and told my mother they'd brought me home.

"Thomas died years ago," the woman said. "He'd taken my car. He didn't know how to drive."

I put the cage down. Then, I turned and ran, heading back to where the car had crashed.

There was no car. No sign of Thomas. One of the trees, an older one, bore scars, as if it had been badly damaged ages ago.

I headed toward the tracks. It was a long walk, but time meant little to me, and fatigue meant nothing.

"That was strange," I whispered. And it was. But it was also good, in a way I'm not sure I can explain. I needed to think about all of this.

But I did know one thing beyond any doubt. For the first time in forever, I felt alive.

THE PRINCIPLE
OF DISCIPLINE

My first week at Santini Middle School, I almost got beaten up by a bully. The kid—I don't even know his name—knocked my books from under my arm when I was on my way to my third-period math class.

"Hey!" I shouted as I spun around to face him. I swallowed whatever else I was going to say, because the kid was big. The way a truck is big next to a car. Or next to a tricycle.

"Be careful." He pushed my shoulder real hard. "Watch where you're going."

This was totally unfair. He'd knocked down my books on purpose, and now he was trying to pick a fight. I figured there was no way I was escaping without getting hurt. I just hoped I could limit the damage to my body so I didn't have to walk around for the next week with a face that looked like uncooked steak. There's nothing better for attracting unwanted attention from bullies than a black eye or a puffed lip. When he started throwing punches, I planned to curl up and cover my head with my arms.

That turned out not to be necessary.

As the bully grabbed my shirt, the principal, Mr. Verger, walked up behind him, put a hand on his shoulder, and said, "Come with me."

Mr. Verger was really big, even compared to the bully. The two of them walked off, like a semi and a dump truck heading down the highway.

"Man, that was close."

I looked over at my friend, Troy, who was standing behind me, about six feet away. "Too close," I said. "I figured I was dead meat."

"I doubt I would have been much help once he started pounding you with his fists," Troy said. "But at least I stuck around."

"Yeah. Thanks." I did appreciate that. I liked to believe I would have done the same thing for him.

"I'm getting sick of these bullies," Troy said.

"Me, too. But I don't think anyone's ever going to do something about them, so we might as well get used to it." I'd sat through dozens of stop-the-bullying assemblies and three or four antibullying movies. It never seemed to make a difference. The bullies just laughed at the assemblies and got new ideas from the movies.

I headed off to class and tried to forget how close I'd come to getting pummeled.

I kept an eye out for that bully the next day, figuring he might be in an even nastier mood after he was punished. He'd probably want to take his anger out on me. But I never saw him again. I didn't think much about it until a month later when I happened to see Principal Verger snag another bully in the hall.

This time, I knew the bully. I knew him way too well. It was

Farley Gormwall. He was pretty mean, but also pretty sneaky. He'd never get in a fight. He'd punch you when nobody was looking, or steal stuff from your backpack when he knew he wouldn't get caught.

I watched Principal Verger lead Farley away after Farley tripped a kid in the hall. That was the last time I saw Farley.

After that, I started to pay more attention to the bully population at Santini. The next time I saw a bully snagged in the hall, it was right before lunch. I followed Principal Verger and the kid. They went into his office. I stopped outside the door. There was no way I could go inside. The secretary would see me. But Principal Verger's office was on the ground floor, and it had a couple windows.

I slipped outside and peeked through his office window. Principal Verger was at his desk, with his back to me. Farley was in a chair on the other side, looking scared and angry.

I couldn't hear what they were saying. But I guess I didn't need to hear anything, because I could see everything. Principal Verger pushed a button that was next to his leg under his desk.

Farley's chair tipped forward. Farley slid off. But he didn't land on the floor. I could see just enough of the floor past the desk to know he'd dropped into some sort of hole. I realized there was a trapdoor in the floor of the principal's office.

I gasped. I guess I was sort of loud, because Principal Verger turned toward the window. I ducked down, then crawled away.

Man. Talk about mixed feelings. I was glad he was getting rid of bullies. But I wasn't sure I liked the way he did it. My feelings didn't stay mixed for long. A week later, when Mike Thamswacker started picking on me, I decided I was totally in favor of Principal Verger's approach to bullying.

Mike was a freak of nature. He was short, but he was frighteningly strong. I'd seen him rip a textbook in half like it was a napkin. And he was the sort of bully who liked to specialize. He'd pick on one person, and torment him until he broke. Somehow, I had become Mike's victim of choice. I guess he'd broken whoever was unlucky enough to have been his previous victim. The school was large enough that I didn't have any idea who it had been.

Now that I was his target, Mike poured motor oil into my locker, stole my pants during gym class and left them in a toilet, poked me in the ribs every chance he got, and put glue on my bicycle seat.

I had to get rid of him. And I knew the perfect way. Principal Verger always walked from his office to the cafeteria at the start of the first lunch period, so he could keep an eye on the kids in the hall. I knew his route. I checked Mike's route. He would be passing right by the corner near room 107 about six seconds before the principal.

I tested this for a whole week. Mike always got there just ahead of the principal. Meanwhile, the torment was getting unbearable. I knew I had to try my plan. The worst that would happen would be that I'd get smacked around. But if things went the way I hoped, Mike would be gone forever.

When the bell rang for lunch period, I ran to room 105, which was empty, and waited inside. When Mike went past, walking toward the corner by room 107, I rushed out and ran right into him from behind. As I bumped him, I saw principal Verger coming the other way.

Perfect.

Except Mike didn't spin around and start tossing out bully threats. He tumbled forward and hit the ground.

"Oowwwww!" He let out a loud cry. Then he rolled over and looked up at me. "Don't hit me again!" he screamed. He put his hands out, as if to hold me off.

"But . . ." Anyone could see he was faking.

A hand clamped down on my shoulder.

"Come with me," Principal Verger said.

"I didn't do anything!" I shouted.

The principal didn't say a word. As he dragged me off, I glanced back. Mike was laughing.

"He's the bully," I said. "You should take Mike to the office."

The principal still ignored me.

"He's been torturing me for weeks." I kept talking, but it was no use. The principal dragged me into his office and tossed me onto the chair that faced his desk.

I popped right out.

"Sit," he said, pointing to the chair.

I looked at the floor in front of the chair. If you didn't know it was there, you'd never spot the outline of the trapdoor. But it was definitely there. "I'd rather stand." I stepped behind the chair.

"Have it your way," he said as he sat at his desk.

"It was an accident," I said. "I was late for class, so I was running."

"I hate bullies," he said.

"I'm not a bully."

"But you know what I hate worse than bullies?" he asked.

I gripped the edge of the chair. "What?"

"Spies," he said. "Sneaky, meddling, prying spies who stick their noses in other people's business." He reached under his desk and pressed something.

The floor behind the chair dropped from beneath my feet. I

guess there was a second trapdoor. I lost my grip on the chair and plunged through the opening. It was a long drop, and it ended with a bad landing. I looked up at the square of light high above my head. Principal Verger stood at the edge of the opening.

"You can't leave me here to die!" I shouted.

"I'm not," he said. "There's food and water. There's just no escape."

Then he moved away, and the trapdoor closed.

My relief that I could somehow survive and maybe find a way out, despite what he'd said, was replaced an instant later by the thought that if I could survive, so could all the others. All the real bullies.

That's when I heard footsteps coming at me from all directions, and realized that, as bad as things seemed right now, they were about to become a whole lot worse.

FWOJTY

That's a heavy head," I said. I gripped it on both sides, and tried to lift it of off the ground. I could barely raise it at all.

"Maybe we should just leave it where it is," my friend Bobby said. "It looks pretty cool, lying there all decapitated."

"Nope. We have to get it up where it belongs," I said. "We put a lot of work into this. We need to finish it."

"You're right, Norm." Jill, Bobby's cousin, stepped next to me and grabbed the head. "On three," she said.

She counted, we lifted, and we managed to get the head in place. It sunk in slightly on the upper body. Good. It would stay in place. I stepped back to admire the results of our efforts.

The timing was perfect.

"Fwosty!" my little brother Ian shouted, pointing at the snowman. He came running over from the path that led down to the lake from the cabins.

"Yeah, Frosty," I said. All week, Ian had been bugging me to make a snowman. I hadn't meant to keep him waiting, but there hadn't been any good, fresh snow until last night, when a foot and a half or so had fallen. It was perfect snow for making a snowman—not too light, not too wet. And I was happy to do something for Ian. He could be a pest, but he was basically okay for a little brother. The pest part mostly happened because he was a huge fan of the whole Frosty thing, about the snowman that comes to life. He watched the video nearly every day, even in the summer, and he sang the song in the car all the way to the lake last week. We come up here every year, during winter break, to ice skate, ski, and ride snowmobiles.

"Make it Fwosty!" Ian shouted. "I got stuff." He ran back to our cabin.

"Fwosty?" Bobby asked.

"From that old video," I said. "You know, the one where the snowman magically comes to life."

"I love that movie," Jill said.

"It would have been better with flame throwers," Bobby said.

I had to agree. "Or zombies," I said. "Reanimated snowmen."

"You can't reanimate something that was never alive," Bobby said.

I couldn't argue with that.

"Scoff!" Ian yelled as he skittered and slid back down the path. A scarf trailed from his raised hand like a poorly designed kite on a dead-calm day.

I grabbed Ian by the waist and lifted him up, so he could wrap the scarf around Fwosty's neck.

We didn't have coal, so I hunted around for stones under the snow. I didn't find any.

"I got this covered," Bobby said. He went to his cabin and came back with a small sack. He pulled out some Oreos, which we used for buttons and broke into pieces to make teeth for a smiling mouth.

"You didn't bring enough for the eyes," I said.

"No problem." He reached back into the sack and extracted two blue tortilla chips that made sort of spooky triangular eyes, like on a jack-o-lantern.

Jill brought a carrot. Her folks were big on salads. Bobby took it and jammed it pointed-end-first into the snowman's face.

"Wrong way," Jill said.

"I like it better," Bobby said. "Speaking of which . . ." He redid some of the cookies, turning the smile into a frown. I glanced over at Ian to make sure he wasn't spooked by the creepy face. He seemed fine with it.

I broke a couple branches off a dead tree that had fallen by the lake, and jammed them into the top of the middle snow boulder for arms.

"Perfect," I said.

"No," Ian said. "He needs the hat."

"We don't have a top hat," I said. "That's what he wears in the movie."

Ian let out a cackle like he knew the greatest joke in the world, and ran to the cabin again.

"Your brother scares me sometimes," Bobby said.

"I think there's some alien DNA way back in my family tree," I said.

Ian returned, carrying a paper bag that seemed way too small to hold a hat. He reached in and pulled out a black disc of some sort.

"Good golly," Jill said. "I think it's a top hat. The old ones collapsed."

"Yeah. I saw that in a movie," Bobby said.

Ian smacked the brim against his open hand a couple times, but he wasn't strong enough to make the hat pop open.

"I'll do it." As I reached out, I asked, "Where'd you get it?"

"From Mr. Lorimar," Ian said, handing me the hat.

I froze. Mr. Lorimar lived two houses down from us. He owned a funeral home. He also owned a used clothing store. All us kids had creepy theories about that. *Chill,* I told myself as I took the hat. I smiled as I realized how appropriate the suggestion was, given the current temperature.

I popped open the hat on my first try. It smelled like the air in the old barbershop my grandfather goes to.

I had to stand on my toes to put the hat on. I still couldn't quite reach.

"I got it," Bobby said. He pushed me aside, then put the hat on Fwosty's head.

I realized Ian was about to get very disappointed. According to the song, it was the hat that made the snowman come to life. I turned toward him and prepared some comforting big-brother words about the difference between fantasy and reality.

"It worked!" Ian shouted. "He comed to life!"

I looked to where Ian pointed, and every organ in my body contracted in an involuntary reaction to stuff that should never happen. Fwosty moved. He turned his head.

I was startled for an instant. But as my organs began to unclench I realized the head was probably just slipping a bit. That realization was shattered as Fwosty swung one of his heavy wooden arms, smacking Bobby across the chest with a whack so loud it made me wince. Bobby went flying at least ten feet.

I screamed and backed up. I could see Bobby was hurt. Fwosty moved closer to him and raised a branch like he was going to impale Bobby right through the heart.

"No!" I shouted. I tackled him.

Sort of.

Not really.

It was more like I nudged him slightly.

I grabbed the raised branch, so I could yank it out of the snow boulder.

Fwosty flung his arm back, throwing me off. He turned away from Bobby and glared at me. Yeah, snack-food eyes can glare. Trust me on this. And hope that you never find out in person.

"Run!" I shouted to Ian and Jill.

I pushed Ian ahead of me, and we took off along the path that circled the lake. The cabins would be safer, if we could get inside, but they were uphill from us. I didn't want to let Fwosty get close to me with those branches.

We ran.

Ian must have been tired from his trips for the scarf and hat. He lagged after we'd run a few yards. I reached down and scooped him up. Or tried to. I slipped on the snow, and my body twisted. I ended up flinging him onto the snow-covered frozen lake. I figured he'd be safe, as long as Fwosty was still chasing me. The ice was thick.

I got back to my feet and ran. Jill froze. Okay, bad word choice. But she stopped running and stared toward Ian. Bad move. I reached to pull her out of the way, but Fwosty clobbered her with a swipe to the gut. She doubled over and went flying. Fwosty turned his attention back to me.

He pointed a branch at me. And, I swear, his tortilla-chip eyes narrowed slightly, as if he had especially painful plans for me. He smacked his arms together. I ran.

I risked a quick glance over my shoulder. Bobby and Jill were both down and out. Neither was moving yet. I checked Ian. He was twitching, like he was having some kind of seizure.

"Ian!" I yelled. "Hold on. I'm coming."

I had to get to him. I spun toward the lake, and nearly had

my head taken off when Fwosty made a hard swipe. I barely managed to lean back far enough to get my head out of the way. The branch buzzed past my face, clipping my shoulder. Fwosty would cut me off if I tried to run to Ian. The best thing I could do was lead him away, and hope that the others could escape.

I headed back along the path around the lake. I was running out of steam. I checked on Ian again. He'd gotten to his feet.

"Go to the cabin!" I shouted.

He took two steps, then fell flat on his back like he'd passed out. He started twitching again.

This was killing me. I needed to get to him. I was his big brother. It was my job to protect him. But Fwosty wanted to beat me down. And once all four of us were down, who knew what the killer snowman would do next? I shuddered as my mind flashed back to the moment when Bobby was almost impaled.

I ran. I gasped for breath. The freezing air ripped at my lungs. My legs ached. I saw Ian try to rise again. He managed another two or three steps before falling.

I staggered as Fwosty smacked my back, right between my shoulder blades. He was catching up. I pumped my legs hard, and gave it everything I had.

And then, I had nothing left to give.

I fell, face-first. I rolled over, but didn't have the strength to get to my feet.

Fwosty caught up with me. From my perspective on the ground, he looked twenty feet tall.

He pointed a branch at my chest. I was about to get pinned to the ground like a butterfly in a museum.

I heard a *whoosh* like a thousand doves had been set loose.

Golden light struck us, freezing Fwosty. Yeah, I know. Word choice, again. But he froze. Then, we both looked up.

Something hovered above us.

An angel—white as new-fallen snow, and small as a child, hovered, sword in hand. Another angel rose from the snow next to Ian, who'd gotten back on his feet. And then, a third.

Angels. Three Ian-sized snow angels, brandishing gleaming golden swords, dove at Fwosty. One sword pierced his chest. A second cleaved him from top hat to bottom orb, splitting him in half. The third went back and forth, dividing the three parts.

The three angels touched their sword tips together, aimed at Fwosty's remains. A stream of fire turned the top hat to ashes and melted the snowman parts. Without a word, or even any sign that they acknowledged our existence, the snow angels flew to the clouds, and beyond.

"You okay?" I asked Ian when I reached him.

"Yeah."

Bobby and Jill staggered over to us.

We stared at each other for a moment.

"You see that?" I asked Bobby.

He nodded. "Smart move, little dude," he said to Ian.

"Let's get out of here," I said. We headed off the lake, skirting widely around the still-steaming puddle of melted snowman.

As we reached the path that led to the cabins, Ian started to sing, "Fwosty, the—"

I tapped him on the shoulder. "Maybe a different song?"

"Okay." He took my hand, and we walked together up the hill.

SERVES YOU RIGHT

So my parents had dragged me and my little sister, Rebekah, on another thrilling family vacation. In other words, we were freezing or burning in the backseat of the car—depending on whether Mom or Dad had control of the air-conditioning at the moment—while mile after mile of perfectly enjoyable countryside zipped past our window. We were on a five-hundred-mile trip to some place that looked exactly like where we were, where we'd been, and where we'd soon be. But the folks had bought a cabin somewhere out there, way way way out there, so that's where we were headed.

Once or twice, just for fun, I asked, "Are we there yet?"

Every time I did that, Mom would glance over her shoulder and say, "Don't annoy your father while he's driving, Katie."

So I'd go back to reading.

"Let's grab some dinner," Dad finally said, when we were halfway between nowhere and somewhere else.

"It's about time," I muttered. Dad didn't like to stop. Not for food, not for bathrooms, not for anything. But I guess even he had to eat, eventually.

"There's a diner," Mom said, pointing ahead to a big silver building with neon lights along the sides and a sign near the road that promised fresh-baked blueberry pies.

"Hardly any cars in the lot," Dad said. "The food can't be very good."

Dad's picky about restaurants. He zoomed past the diner. He also zoomed past the next three places we saw, including one that offered giant, frosty milkshakes and char-grilled burgers.

Mom tried to find a restaurant using her phone, but she's hopeless at that, and she refuses to let me do it for her.

Finally, Dad pulled into a parking lot at a restaurant called The Kreepy Cafe. Under the sign, in smaller letters, I saw: ICKY FUN FOR THE WHOLE FAMILY. "Icky" and "fun" didn't strike me as natural partners.

I got out and stretched. I was starving. I took Rebekah's hand and followed my parents inside. The place was really dark, with fake—I hoped—cobwebs hanging from the ceiling, and creepy organ music wavering in the background. The guy at the register was wearing a lot of eye shadow, like someone playing a vampire in a low-budget movie. I felt the urge to give him a lesson in how to apply makeup.

"Four?" he asked.

"Four," Dad said.

"Walk this way." He chuckled after he said it, like it was some kind of joke.

We followed him to a table in a dark corner of a dark dining room. He handed Mom and Dad big menus shaped like coffins, and then gave me and Rebekah children's menus shaped like spiders. It was hard to see the menu in the dark. I squinted at the page, expecting the usual hot dog, grilled cheese, and hamburger that seem to haunt every kid's menu at every restaurant I've ever been to. Instead, I saw stuff like this:

Wormghetti with clot balls

Chicken Needle Soup

Harmburger

Killed cheese sandwich

Severed chicken fingers

And so on. Some of the items were served with "French flies" and "cole slaughter."

Next to me, Rebekah, who was just starting to read, said, "Ewwwww," and dropped the menu, as if the spider had come to life and started wriggling in her hands.

I let out my own little ewwww, then said, "This is disgusting. Can I order from the adult menu?"

Dad glanced over at my menu. "Oh, come on. It's just a joke. 'Wormghetti' is just going to be spaghetti. And the clot balls will be meatballs. You know that."

"It's still kind of sickening," I said.

"Would you rather not eat?" Mom asked. "You can sit and watch us, if that's what you want."

I could see I wasn't going to win this argument. "I'll find something."

The waiter, who was as badly made up as the host, came to take our orders.

"I'll have the spaghetti," I said.

"Wormghetti," he said, writing my order on his pad.

"Whatever." I wasn't going to play that game.

Rebekah ordered the killed-cheese sandwich. She looked like she was about ready to cry.

"You don't have to eat it," I whispered to her.

"But I'm hungry," she said.

"I'm in the mood for steak," Dad said. "I'll have the eye round."

That made me even angrier. Mom cooked eye round for us once in a while, and it was really tasty. I liked it even better than sirloin or flank steak. It wasn't fair that Dad got a steak and I didn't. But there wasn't any steak on the kid's menu.

"I'll have the Hungarian goulash," Mom said.

As the waiter left, Mom turned to me and said, "You will eat every bite on your plate. No arguments. Understand?"

"Yes, Mom."

"Every bite," Dad said. "That's the rule for this meal."

"Yes, Dad."

Rebekah squeezed my hand. I squeezed back, trying to reassure her that everything would be okay. When the waiter came with the food and put my plate down in front of me, I was relieved to see that the wormghetti really was just spaghetti. And the clot balls were meatballs. Rebekah's killed-cheese sandwich was just grilled cheese, nice and gooey, with golden-brown buttery toast.

"Okay?" I whispered to her.

"Okay," she whispered back.

I twirled some spaghetti on my fork.

That's when I heard my parents gasp. They were staring down at their plates.

I picked up the adult menu and took a look. I guess my parents didn't pay too much attention to what they were reading in the dim light. Mom's dinner was listed as "Hungarian Ghoulash," which is definitely not the same as goulash, and Dad's meal was described as "eyes 'round a steak."

Dad's steak was surrounded with eyeballs, staring up at him. Mom's stew had some ghoulish things peeking out of it, like shards of bone and strips of worm-infested meat.

"Every bite," I said as I cut a meatball in half. I raised my eyes from my plate and forced myself to watch my parents eat. I knew it would make me feel a bit sick to see what they were cutting, chewing, and swallowing. But it would also make me happy.

BLOOD DONORS

eak.
So weak.

If I don't get some blood soon, I will die.

No. Wrong word. Undead can't die. Still . . . I'd perish. I think that's a distinction without a difference. Either way, it won't be pleasant. I witnessed the perishing of an undead, once. He'd broken our most sacred law, speaking to a mortal about our ancient history, revealing our strengths and weaknesses. Rather than cast him into daylight, the council chose to let him perish from lack of blood. Sunlight is a painful, searing end, but it is quick. Starvation means days of suffering.

We can hibernate. Again, not the right word for our dormancy, but it will do. Some have passed decades entombed. But we can only survive like that in a coffin of our native soil.

They'd destroyed his coffin and scattered the soil. Then they kept him confined until he was nearly finished, moaning for mercy, begging for blood.

They'd released him in an alley, in the dark of night, to crawl,

163

knowing blood was nearby, too weak to take any. He was too weak to call a mortal to him. Too weak, even, to call a dog, or a rat. The smaller the creature, the less will is required. He lacked the strength to draw anything to him.

We all watched. We were ordered us to observe. They wanted us to clearly see and understand the lesson. The rules are in place for a reason. Rules, order, obedience. That is how we have survived undetected among the warmbloods for so many centuries.

Now, I had violated one of those rules. I thought I'd been careful. I thought I'd hidden my work. But somehow they discovered my experiments. We've always had control of certain mammals, especially wolves and bats. And rats, of course. I'd wanted to extend our power.

My kind does not like progress or innovation. They are frightfully, and maddeningly, bound by tradition. There are some of us who disagree. I've had centuries to read the great books and letters of those scientists who've advanced the mortals' knowledge about themselves and the world around us. Without these innovators, we'd still be walking through the gas-lit coal smog of London, or crouching in caves.

So there I was. Imprisoned while I starved. When they opened the door to fetch me, I couldn't even stand. I could barely even raise my head. They carried me to the street. The sun had just set. I'd have hours to lie, suffering. Our hunger is not like that of mortals. It enters every cell and fiber of our body. It is a longing, both mental and physical, that shreds the mind and eclipses all else. We become our hunger.

They stepped back after they'd tossed me to the ground. Watching. Some seemed pleased. Others, those who supported me, seemed saddened, at least to that small extent which we feel emotions. But they knew they couldn't come to my aid. We can never go to war with ourselves. This we learned from the mortals.

I will not perish without a struggle. My work is too important.

So hungry . . .

I wasn't in an alley. They placed me in a yard, near a wooden fence. I knew this was done to taunt me and heighten my suffering, because I could hear life on the other side. I reached with my mind, and found blood passing by on the busy street. But I couldn't turn the humans to my will. I was desperately weak.

A rat scuttled past. I tried with all my remaining strength to summon him.

He barely slowed. And then, he was gone.

I shifted my thoughts in ways I'd mastered during the past five years of research. I called out.

They came.

So small. Unseen by those who are not looking. But subject to my will.

They swarmed.

Mosquitoes. Small blood suckers.

Each brought to my thirsting mouth a tiny fraction of a drop of blood. It seemed an eternity before there was even enough to swallow. Finally, the first partial mouthful trickled down my throat. I felt my body respond. I lay still, not revealing my struggle back from the edge of extinction to the crowd of onlookers.

Another eternity, another swallow, and then another. It was nowhere near enough to give me the strength to rise, but it was enough to allow me the strength to summon two large rats.

I grabbed one in each hand, and drained them in an instant.

There was still hunger. But there was also strength.

I rose and turned toward those who condemned me. As did my allies.

The war began.

ABRA-CA-DEBORAH

How long before someone says it? Deborah wondered as she carried her equipment through the backstage entrance. She paused to study the crowd hustling around the dimly lit area and decided it would be less than a minute before she heard those familiar words. Bracing for the inevitable, Deborah took a deep breath, savoring the familiar mingled aromas of shellacked hardwood floors and musty velvet curtains.

Someone spoke the expected words before Deborah had a chance to exhale.

"Hey, what's she doing here? She's a girl."

Deborah stared at the speaker. He was a grubby little boy, maybe five or six years old, dressed in a miniature tuxedo with a too-large top hat on his too-large head. A red clip-on bow tie appeared and disappeared beneath the loose flesh of his wagging jaw like an upside-down version of a bobbing apple. His face had been scrubbed and polished, but he still looked grubby. His mother, who was straightening the top hat, made a minor attempt to shush him, but he continued to broadcast his opinions.

"Girls don't do magic. Magic is for boys." The last word came out sounding like "boyzes."

I was right, Deborah said to herself, *less than a minute and they've started.* She'd have guessed the first snub would have come from one of the boys her own age, but it didn't surprise her that a younger boy had spoken up. She felt all the other eyes shift toward her. The boys, as nervous as they must have been, turned away from their cards and doves and rabbits for a moment to glare at this girl who dared to practice their craft. She was used to boys acting this way, but Deborah expected better from the mothers. They were women. They should have known how it felt. They should have understood. But they joined their sons and stared at her with the scowl reserved for invaders of sacred turf.

"Girls don't do magic," the boy said again, looking up toward his mother.

The mother gave a small nod.

"This girl does magic," Deborah said, speaking quietly, and more to herself than to the angry figures that stared at her. She wove her way to the far wall, knowing most of the eyes were still following her. *I'm glad I didn't wear the dress,* she thought. That would have given them even more to stare at. Deborah knew she looked enchanting in the evening gown. She could be enchanting—that was no problem. But she'd decided to go with a modest blouse and black slacks. When she got onstage, she wanted to be judged on her skills. She didn't want to score points based on any gifts of birth.

As Deborah reached the corner farthest from the stage, she could hear drifting bits of whispered exchanges. Bursts of locker-room laughter rose from random spots as boys made their stupid comments. Deborah fought her urge to strike out at them. It would be so easy to let her rage win. For a moment, she savored the thought of lashing back. But that wasn't why she'd come. The North American Magician's Association was the largest magic organization in the country. If she could win the junior contest, she knew people would have to take her seriously. This was her last chance for the juniors—once she turned thirteen, she'd have to compete with the adults. And as much as she dreamed of winning first place in the adult division, she knew that it was a whole different world from the juniors.

Deborah blocked out the lingering chatter as she set down her kit. Unlike the boys, she'd come alone. Her mother had left the city on business last night, taking another of her many midnight flights.

"Break a leg, kid," she'd said when she'd given Deborah a hug for luck. "But make sure it isn't one of yours."

Deborah didn't mind looking after herself. She wasn't lonely. She had her cat at home, and her books.

As she prepared her equipment, she scanned the room, trying to spot the real competition. From the props she saw and the practice moves the boys were running through, there didn't seem to be anyone she couldn't beat, based on talent alone. But, at shows like these, talent never stood alone. The little kid would be a problem. The judges always favored the youngest contestants, even if they had no real talent. A small kid badly performing simple tricks from a cheap magic kit could almost always score better than an experienced twelve-year-old performing difficult effects. Other than the little kid, Deborah saw nothing to worry her. Most of the contestants were just hobbyists.

It won't hurt to give them a bit of a scare, Deborah thought. She reached into her kit and took out a deck of cards. The deck disappeared. Then it reappeared. She fanned the deck with one hand, spreading the cards smoothly. The deck, still fanned, disappeared again, only to reappear one card at a time. Not bad, she thought. There weren't many kids her age who could back-palm a whole deck. There weren't even that many adults who could perform the sleight this smoothly.

I'm good, Deborah told herself. *I'm very good.*

Still, this one flourish wasn't enough to make her stand out as the very best. Deborah took the effect a step further. She held up another deck in her left hand. Making a special effort to ignore her audience of sons and mothers, she repeated the sequence, but this time she did it with both hands at once. Cards appeared and disappeared with grace and flare. Months of practice, hours each day in front of a mirror, were the only secret here.

"Man, she's good," someone whispered.

"Ssshhh," someone else said. "She's not that good."

Keeping her expression neutral, Deborah stashed the cards in her pocket and picked up a green sponge ball from her kit. She rolled it across her fingers, savoring the way it waltzed on the dance floor of her hand. She tossed the ball up in the air, then caught it. She tossed it again. It changed color. She tossed it a third time. One ball rose into the air—two balls fell. She repeated the sequence with both hands. "Just a girl," she said to no one in particular. *I'm a lot more than just a girl,* she thought, allowing herself a small smile, *but they'll never know the real me.*

Something else grabbed Deborah's attention. She dropped the sponge balls back into her kit as the announcer walked in and spoke to the contestants. "Okay, kids, let's get this show going." He read off the order of appearance from a sheet on a clipboard. Deborah was next to last. That was a good sign. In the old days, the top act—the headliner—always went on next to last. Deborah wondered whether any of the boys in the room had ever bothered to study the history of their art. The position near the end also allowed Deborah to see almost all of her competition before she performed. The snotty little kid was the only one who would go on after her.

"I want a soda," he said to his mother.

Speaking of little brats, Deborah thought as she glanced over at him.

"Quiet, Abner," his mother said, "the show is starting."

"I WANT A SODA!" he shouted, his mouth getting large enough to eclipse half his face.

"Yes, darling," his mother said, digging frantically in her purse for change. "Mommy will get you a soda." She hurried off.

Deborah shook her head. This kid was a real brat. She turned her back on him and joined the fringes of the crowd as they watched the show from the side of the stage. The first kid wasn't bad, but he was obviously a beginner. He looked nervous, and he didn't know how to use the microphone. He kept talking as he moved around, so his voice would fade in and out. Deborah knew the judges would kill him for that mistake. They said Houdini had the lung power to work without a microphone—but this kid wasn't Houdini. The next two acts weren't any better, or any worse. Each boy did a few tricks he'd probably just bought off the shelf at a magic shop. Each boy received polite applause.

But Deborah loved magic so much, she didn't even mind watching beginner magic. There was something she could learn from any performance. And there was something wonderful about the art. Deborah found great beauty in creating the illusion of magic through skill and cunning. And, despite what these kids said or thought, there had been many successful female magicians. But mostly, women were stuck walking around in ridiculous costumes, wiggling their flesh while handing out swords and taking away doves.

Deborah's dream was to change all that. Nobody was going to saw *her* in half. She wanted to become the world's most famous female magician. *Not just female*, she reminded herself as she thought about her goal. She wanted to become the world's most famous magician, period. And she wanted to do it through hard work, practice, and skill. *No tricks or shortcuts for me*, she thought as she watched another act. The kid was doing some fancy flourishes with a deck of cards, but it was a trick deck where the cards were threaded together. Deborah knew that any good magician in the audience would immediately spot the gimmick. And the judges were all excellent magicians with years of experience. Deborah wasn't going to take the easy way. No gimmicks, no fancy equipment, no special help of any kind.

She watched the next boy. He moved well. Deborah suspected he had a natural talent—but not for magic. He might have made a wonderful dancer, or maybe a mime. He made an adequate magician, but she knew he'd never rise beyond the level of birthday parties and talent shows. Deborah shook her head—she understood quite well that the talent a person was given at birth wasn't always the talent that brought happiness. She had other skills, herself, but magic was where her dream lay.

"You're next," the announcer told her as the boy onstage finished his act with a decent version of the torn-and-restored newspaper routine.

This was when the real butterflies always hit. Deborah knew

the panic would fade the moment she started to perform. But for now, she had to live with the spasms that rippled through her stomach. She rushed back and grabbed her kit from the far corner where she'd left it, then walked onto the stage. As always, the instant she felt the bright lights above her head and the hardwood floor beneath her feet she knew this was where she belonged. She set her kit on top of a stool and reached inside for the silk handkerchief she used for her first effect.

A cold shock stopped her.

Deborah's fingertips dipped into a slimy mess. Bubbles tingled against her skin.

"What . . . ?"

She stood frozen for a moment, not understanding. Then she knew. Realization and anger flooded her at the same time. Someone had poured soda on her equipment. Everything was a sticky disaster. There was nothing she could do. There was no quick way to repair the damage. It was beyond her power. A high-pitched giggle struck at her from the wings. Deborah saw the little beast peering at her from the shadows at the side of the stage. He bounced from foot to foot, almost dancing in delight.

Deborah wanted to strike back. But the audience was waiting. She could sense them nearing that moment when a crowd's attention turns from excitement to boredom or—worse yet— to pity. Another instant, and she knew she'd lose them. In the few minutes allowed for each act, there was no way she'd ever win them back if she let them slip away now.

The cards! She had two decks in her pocket. Deborah wiped her hand on her pants, then reached into her pocket. *Be your best*, she thought. As soon as her fingers felt the familiar surface of the pasteboards, she slipped into her rhythm—each hand dancing a slow waltz with fifty-two life-long friends. Within seconds, the crowd was captured by her spell—a spell woven from nothing but two hands and two decks of cards.

They were hers. She was magic.

Nothing stood in her way. Every flourish was perfect, every effect was flawless. As she reached her ending, Deborah knew she had stunned them with her skill. Feeling like a figure skater approaching her hardest jump, she pointed to a man in the audience. "Name a card."

"Six of clubs," the man said.

She pointed to a woman. "Another card, please."

"Jack of hearts," the woman said.

Deborah repeated the names, then threw the two decks into the air, above her head. As the cards rained down, she thrust her hands into the fluttering cloud. Then she lifted her hands high in triumph, the six of clubs grasped in her right hand, the jack of hearts in her left.

Perfect, she thought. *It was perfect.*

Deborah smiled and bowed. The audience went wild. They clapped and cheered and stomped their feet. The sound embraced her like her mother's hugs. Even some of the boys watching from the wings clapped for her. Deborah waited until the applause showed the first signs of dying, then bowed again and turned to leave the stage.

"Girls aren't magicians?" she whispered, smiling even wider.

She said it again as she moved behind the curtain, hurling the words like a missile at one small target.

"Big deal," the boy said as Deborah glided past him. "Watch me." He strutted onto the stage, puffed like a rooster who thinks the hen house is the entire world.

Deborah knew he couldn't be any good. He had too much hatred inside of him to be a real magician. Magic was born of calm and confidence. But she was still worried. The judges could fall for him because he was little.

He started off well. The crowd liked him, even though he was less skilled than any of the other boys. He made coins appear and disappear. He did it just poorly enough that Deborah was sure the judges thought he was cute.

Deborah studied the judges. They were grinning and nodding at each other. One judge whispered to the man next to him. From where she stood, it looked like he'd said, "Isn't he adorable?"

For a moment, Deborah closed her eyes and squeezed her hands into fists, reminding herself of her vow. She would win through skill and not trickery. She wouldn't win with gimmicks or by draping herself in a slinky dress or using any unfair powers. Deborah wanted an honest victory.

You don't always get what you want, she reminded herself as she watched the little kid. *And life is rarely fair.*

Deborah told herself she should just wait and take her chances. But the boy had played a rotten trick on her. She couldn't help aiming bad thoughts toward him. He was so nasty that some of what he'd done to her would surely have to come back around eventually and bite him. Deborah just wanted the biting to start right away.

"Drop them," Deborah whispered. She unclenched her fists.

There was a clatter as the boy dropped a handful of hidden coins. He made a joke about it. The crowd laughed. He started his next trick. He cut a rope in half. "Mess up, you little brat," Deborah whispered.

The boy waved his hand over the rope. It was still in two pieces. He looked puzzled, but he made another joke. The crowd laughed, but not as hard as before.

It got worse. Every trick went wrong. Toward the end, even Deborah felt sorry for the brat. But, as the announcer called her onstage to take her trophy for first place, she stopped thinking about the boy altogether.

In her hands, the trophy was like a cup that could hold unlimited dreams and hopes. It was hers, and she had earned it. Her vow, though bruised, remained unbroken.

As she left the stage, she saw him again. His top hat was on the floor, crushed under his foot. His bow tie had been flung across the room. He looked up at her and said, "You just won 'cause you're a girl." His mother was not in sight. Deborah figured she was probably off on another errand for her little darling.

"Girls aren't magicians," the boy told her.

Deborah bent down close to him and put her mouth next to his ear. "That's going to change," she said quietly. She hesitated, glanced around, then said one thing more. "And you forgot something, you stupid little boy. Maybe you think girls aren't magicians. But even a silly little brat like you must know that some girls are witches. I couldn't fix the mess you made of my equipment. I'm not that powerful, yet. But making someone turn clumsy—that's not hard at all. I could do that when I was three. I can do even more now." She touched his lips with her right forefinger and whispered a final word.

"Silence."

Then she laughed and walked away.

She almost felt pity for him. Without looking back, she knew he was standing there with his mouth open and his face frozen in surprise. For the moment, the world would be spared from having to hear him. His voice would come back in an hour or two. As for his clumsiness, Deborah suspected it would last a while longer. Eventually, it might wear off. But, for the moment, it looked like some boys weren't destined to be magicians, either.

THE QUILTY CLOWN

The life of the average six-month-old baby is pretty sweet. Quentin, who was slightly above average in many ways, but still just an infant, was no exception. He got fed, he got hugged, and he got loved. Life was definitely sweet. At least, that's how it was before the quilty clown showed up.

He heard about it, first, before he saw it. Quentin couldn't talk all that much, yet. Mostly, he burbled and cooed. He hadn't figured out how to make all of the sounds his parents made, and he was still learning what words were all about. But he understood what he heard.

Dinga-chinga-dinga-bing.

That was the doorbell. Quentin loved hearing the bell. It was like music. And it meant someone was coming for a visit. Visitors were wonderful. They leaned over his crib and smiled. They adored him. They tickled his belly and sang songs to him.

"Hello, dearie."

Quentin smiled. He knew that voice, even when the speaker was all the way across the house. Faraway voices were softer.

But this one was still recognizable. It was Mrs. Pepson, from across the street.

"Hello," his mother said. "What do you have there?"

"Something for the precious little one," Mrs. Pepson said. "I saw it at a garage sale, and I just knew your little boy would love it."

For me, Quentin thought. Even though he didn't hear his name, he knew he was also *the little boy*. He burbled. He wanted to say, "Yay!" but he hadn't quite mastered that word, yet. Besides, burbling conveyed his feelings perfectly adequately.

He heard footsteps coming his way. Sounds got louder when they got closer. His mom and Mrs. Pepson reached the crib.

"Look, Quentin," his mom said, holding something up. "Mrs. Pepson brought this for you. Isn't it wonderful?"

Quentin laughed and clapped his hands. His mom was holding a quilt. It was filled with bright colors. Quentin knew all about quilts, since he slept with one that covered him and kept him snug, and he took naps on the couch on another one that his grandma had made for him.

But this quilt was different. Instead of squares and triangles, it was a clown—a big, smiling clown, with a huge red mouth, a red-and-blue-striped shirt, white gloves, yellow pants, and enormous black shoes. One raised hand clutched strings tied to a bunch of balloons. The other hand pointed straight out, as if to say, "These are for you." The quilt was stretched over a frame.

"I know just where to put it," his mom said. She walked to the wall opposite his crib and took down the painting of three men in a tub that hung there. Then she hung up the quilted clown, gave Quentin a kiss, and left the room. Quentin liked the men in the tub, but he'd seen them all of his life, so he was ready for something different.

Quentin watched the clown, and smiled. He was happy all morning and afternoon. He was happy for part of the evening—until the clown smiled back.

It wasn't a nice smile, like the clown had worn until now. It was a mean smile. And it didn't happen until the sun set and the room grew dark. Quentin lived in a house on a corner where two busy streets crossed. Every time a car drove past his house, the headlights would shine in through his bedroom window, sweeping across the wall.

As another pair of headlights highlighted the smile, which had grown larger and scarier, Quentin screamed. His mom and dad came running into the room. They flipped on the lamp next to his crib.

"What's wrong?" his mom asked.

Quentin hated this question, because there was never any way he could answer it. No matter what was wrong—hungry stomach, wet diaper, itchy bottom—he didn't know how to make the words that would explain the problem.

He wanted to scream, "Get that clown out of here!" But he lacked the skills to do that. So he pointed and howled.

"I think he's scared of the clown," his dad said.

"He couldn't be," his mom said. "He loved it. You should have seen how his face lit up when I showed it to him. He watched it all day. He loves the clown."

"No I don't!" Quentin wanted to scream.

His mom picked Quentin up, whispered, "Hush," and rubbed his back.

Quentin was powerless against that sort of magic. Despite his fears, he fell asleep and didn't wake until the next morning.

Across the room, hanging from the wall, the clown looked safe and cheerful in the early sunlight. The evil smile was gone.

Quentin wondered if anything had actually happened last night. He was still getting used to seeing and hearing things. And he was often wrong about what he thought he was experiencing. He didn't quite understand how his father made his whole face disappear when he played the peek-a-boo game or how the pictures appeared and disappeared on the television. And things were tricky to watch in the moving beams of headlights that danced across his walls at night. So maybe there was nothing evil about the clown.

He changed his mind when night fell.

The clown gave him the same evil smile. Things grew rapidly worse after that. Even in the dim light between the cars, Quentin could see the quilt jerk, as if someone inside were pulling down at it. The frame bumped the wall, but not loudly enough to wake his parents. More bumps followed, like the beating of a slow heart. Then, Quentin heard another sound that was far worse.

Rip.

The clown's raised arm tore free of the cloth on either side.

The arm reached across toward the opposite shoulder, grabbed a fistful of quilt, and yanked.

Rip.

Quentin howled.

His parents rushed in. The clown's free hand slipped back where it belonged. As his mom picked him up and soothed him, his father said, "I hope this isn't some new thing. Please tell me he won't wake us up every night."

"It's just a phase," his mother said as she rubbed Quentin's back and swayed from side to side. "All babies go through phases."

Quentin's head started to droop. As it flopped down, he caught a glimpse of the grinning clown.

He's going to get me.

Quentin let his whole body go limp, as if he were already asleep. It was the first time he attempted an act of deception. At the same time he pretended to be asleep, he also struggled to stay awake. His mom gave his back several gentle pats, bringing him dangerously close to drifting off, then lifted him from her shoulder.

"There we go," she said. "He's fast asleep."

She put him back in the crib. He'd done it. He'd managed to stay awake. Quentin lay still, pretending to be asleep. The idea that he could fool his parents amazed him. But he had more important things to think about right now. He opened his eyes the tiniest slit, to watch the wall.

The clown reached up, again, and pulled at his shoulder. He was ripping himself from the quilt, one stitch at a time. The shoulder and arm came free.

The clown grabbed his head with two hands, scrunching the material of his forehead, and pulled downward. In a moment, he'd torn his whole upper body out of the quilt.

He flopped down and worked on his legs, like someone unlacing tall boots.

Quentin screamed again.

The door opened. "Oh, good heavens, Quentin, go to sleep," his mom said.

"We should go in," his dad said.

"No," his mom said. "The books say that sometimes you just have to let them cry. It's hard. But it's the right thing to do."

"We might as well try that," his dad said. "We have nothing to lose."

The door closed.

The clown dropped to the floor as the last stitches broke. He hit with a thud that sounded heavier than it should have.

Quentin watched the clown crawl across the floor toward the crib. It reached the leg near Quentin's head and started to climb up toward the rails.

"Oh, baby," the clown whispered. Its voice was like gravel and steel.

It climbed higher up the leg. The passage was slow on the slippery, polished wood. But the clown was making progress.

"I'm going to hug you tight," the clown said. "Right around your neck."

Quentin screamed, then looked at the door. He listened for footsteps.

Nothing.

No sign of rescue.

Quentin, pushed by fear and a survival instinct, began his first complex chain of thoughts.

I have to keep the clown from reaching me.

How?

He watched the clown inch up the leg of the crib.

Heavy things are hard to lift.

The clown needed to be too heavy to climb. But it wasn't.

I need to make it heavier.

What made things heavy?

Quentin thought about his diaper. When it was dry, it was light. When it got wet, it was heavy. He clutched his bottle and turned it upside down. The water wouldn't come out.

A white gloved hand grabbed the bottom of the rail. "Got your nose," the clown said. "Not yet. But soon."

How did his mom open the bottle?

"Rip it right off," the clown said. "Ouchies!"

Quentin shut his eyes and pictured her twisting the top.

A second hand grabbed the rails. "Baby go bye-bye," the clown whispered.

It was hard. Quentin wasn't sure how to do it. But somehow, he got the top loose.

He tipped the bottle and poured the water on the quilty clown just as the dreadful head rose into sight above the mattress and the smile stretched so wide, it became a red slash across the clown's entire face.

Soaked, the clown slid back down the leg to the floor. It spouted angry words and made a few attempts to climb back up the slick surface, but then lay limply on the floor, as if exhausted.

Look! I did it myself!

That's what Quentin wanted to scream. But he knew nobody would come, tonight. And even if they did, nobody would understand the burbled half-formed words. As Quentin slipped back to sleep, he had another surprise. But this one was pleasant and full of promise. He discovered he could finally say, "Yay!"

His parents came in the morning. They stared, they talked, they made guesses to explain the inexplicable, and they failed to understand. But they took the clown away, and put it in the garbage, where it belonged.

A WORD OR TWO ABOUT THESE STORIES

Since writers are always being asked, "Where do you get your ideas?" I like to end each collection with some insights into my inspirations. It's best to read this after you finish the stories, since there will be some spoilers.

Easy Targets

Charter schools were in the news a lot when I was working on this collection, as were stories about violence in schools. This led me to think about schools as safe environments. It wasn't hard to go from there to thinking about a school specifically designed to have no bullies, which led me to think about what would happen if there was one bully in that school. Which led, as you've seen, to taking the idea one step further.

Parasites

I really did hear that poem when I was a kid. I've written other stories about this sort of concept, where there are levels of things, most notably in "Bad Luck," from *The Battle of the Red Hot Pepper Weenies*, where the guy who is in charge of causing bad luck discovers that he, too, can become a victim of bad luck. But I think this is one of my favorites. I like that I can put stories with a wide variety of moods into these collections. I suspect some readers might object to the idea that vampires have blood. In some stories, they don't. In others, they do. I guess I'll just have to ask the next vampire I meet to settle things for me.

Frozen in Time

One of the great luxuries given to me as a story writer is that I can explore all sorts of structures, concepts, techniques, and literary devices. Ideas that might be too risky to use for a whole novel are perfect for short stories. (More about that when I discuss "Dominant Species.") There are certain concepts that have been trotted out over and over for stories. These are called *tropes*. A trope can be a cliché, but it can also be fun to play with. Getting a message from your future self is definitely a trope. But I think I managed to turn it into an amusing story. I hope you agree.

In Warm Blood

The sanguine idea for the ending came first. It's a fairly basic concept—letting the hunter become the victim. Once I knew how I wanted it to end, it wasn't hard to figure out the rest of the story. Sometimes, I'll get an idea for an ending that is fairly hard to orchestrate. Let's say, to use a wild, hypothetical example, I have an idea that requires my character to end up climbing a tree while holding a pickle in his mouth and a checkerboard under his arm. That's going to be a tough story to write. If you work too hard to set up an ending, or make the characters do unlikely things, the ending will feel contrived. That's not good. By the way, there's been a bit of debate recently over whether dinosaurs were warm- or cold-blooded. But given that the air was hot, I could safely describe the blood as warm either way. And there's a bit of debate about the distinction between the brontosaurus and the apatosaurus. At least if there's a mistake about that, it's Kenneth's error and not mine.

Interestingly enough, just as I was going over the final edits for this book, a new largest dinosaur was discovered. I considered changing the story so it mentioned the titanosaur, but I realized there will inevitably be other, larger discoveries. So I decided to leave things alone.

The Duggly Uckling

Ever since I wrote "The Princess and the Pea Brain" for *The Battle of the Red Hot Pepper Weenies*, I try to make sure each collection has a fractured fairy tale. The idea for this one came straight from the title. As you may know, that sort of wordplay where the opening letters of words are swapped is called a Spoonerism. Puns, Spoonerisms, and other types of wordplay are great starting points for ideas. If you are having a hard time finding an idea for a story, look at the titles of fairy tales, songs, or even paintings, and see what your mind does with the words.

Spell Binding

I try to write a "what if" question every day. Many of my stories come from that. In this case, the "what if" was, "What if a wizard used a spell book as a trap to defeat a rival?" Naturally, the idea could have been spun out into a wide variety of stories. It could have focused on the rival (as did "The Wizard's Mandolin" from *The Battle of the Red Hot Pepper Weenies*). But this is the variation that caught my fancy.

Strikeout of the Bleacher Weenies

When my daughter was young, she played on various rec-league teams. There was always a handful of parents (and, sadly, even some coaches) who took things far too seriously. Whenever I thought about possible Weenies title stories, that was one concept that came to mind. But the story itself came together in bits and pieces. I knew there'd be an opening scene with some sort of sport being played. Originally, I thought about soccer, but when the word "strikeout" came to me as part of the title, I realized the story would probably have to be about baseball, at least in part. And when I saw Bill Mayer's amazing cover art, that cemented things. The idea for the ending came next. In the original idea, the story stopped when the Bleacher Weenies got carried off for their reward. But it felt wrong to do that to a bunch of parents, even if they'd behaved pretty badly. As I was thinking about this, the idea for the last scene, and the whole thing about "losing heart," came to mind, and I knew I could now make the penultimate (I love that word) scene as grisly as I wanted without making the story too scary or depressing. The added kicker about "sacrifice" hit me as I was doing a revision pass. (In case you are wondering, I do a lot of revision passes on these stories. Most of them have been revised at least fifteen or twenty times before I'm finished with them.)

Camping Out

I went camping. Once. That was enough for me. But I got a lot of ideas from that experience, including the plot for a title story, "The Curse of the Campfire Weenies." (Side note: I wrote that story because my brilliant editor, Susan Chang, felt that a camping scene would make a great cover.) When I started out writing about the girl on the camping trip, all I knew was I liked the idea of someone waking up in a tent and discovering she was alone. When I set the character on the trail, I had no idea what would happen. As much as it's a good idea to plan a story and to do an outline, sometimes it's fun to just start writing and see where your imagination takes you. Just don't forget to bring a flashlight, so you can see what's lurking in the darkest corners of your mind.

Dominant Species

I read an article about the fungus that appeared to be a lot of small growths but was actually one huge life form. That led me to think about other things that are spread across the land, which led me to sand. This story is a good example of how varied the narrative voice and viewpoint can be in different stories in a collection. It's also a great example of how short stories are the perfect way to explore things that would be difficult to pull off in a novel. Basically, I wrote a story about sand, told by an omniscient narrator, after which you read a story about sand. If I wrote a novel about sand, I suspect nobody would ever get to read it.

Swing Round

I've heard about the inside-out thing ever since I was a kid. (Yes, we had swings way back then. They were made with rocks and vines, but they worked pretty well until the mastodons chased us off the playground.) And I am fond of young scientists. (If you share my admiration for young scientists, check out the Nathan Abercrombie, Accidental Zombie books. Nathan's friend Abigail is an awesome science genius.) This is another case where I started writing with no idea what would happen. That gets easier with practice. I don't recommend doing this too often when you're starting out. It's good to have a road map. But I've written so many short stories, over so many years, I feel pretty comfortable hitting the road without a GPS.

All the Tricks

I was a magic geek when I was in elementary and middle school. (You can see a totally geeky photo of me performing if you go to the biography in the personal section of my Web page, www.davidlubar.com.) I remember going to a magic show at the high school auditorium back when I was around ten years old, and feeling pretty smug that I knew how most of the tricks were done. I really wanted to be the kid who got called onstage to help with a trick. It's probably a good thing I wasn't picked. I suspect at best I would have been pretty annoying and, at worst, I would have made a total fool of myself. Those memories inspired the story. As an adult, I can look at that sort of situation from the perspective of the magician. That's what inspired the ending.

enDANGERed

I wanted to write a scene where people are melting down silver so they can hunt a werewolf. (And, for anyone wondering how I came up with ninety-seven pieces, don't forget that backgammon includes two dice and a doubling cube.) The original story started off with a very moody feel. But the story took a twist during the final scenes, and I found myself with a lighthearted ending that didn't match the rest of the story at all. I had two choices. I could find a different ending with a moody feel, or I could keep the ending and make the rest of the story lighter. As tough as it was to give up an opening I felt was nicely crafted, I liked the ending. Moody, literary prose tends to get more respect, and is viewed as having more value, but humor is actually a lot harder to write. (This is an opinion, not a fact.)

Just for fun, I figured I'd share a bit of the original, unedited opening. It would have been very jarring to follow something like this with a funny ending.

My mother looked like she was going to cry when Dad melted down her favorite candlestick. I'd heard rumors and whispers for weeks, but until that moment, I hadn't really believed any of this was real.

"What's going on?" I asked him.

"It's nothing, Sabrina." He put a hand on my shoulder and smiled, then went back to pouring the molten metal into the molds. I would have felt better if I hadn't felt his arm tremble.

"You're making silver bullets," I said. "Why?"

"It's just something I have to do," he said.

I looked over at Mom. She was trying to be brave, too. I guess she was fighting both the sadness of her loss—she'd loved those candlesticks—and the fear of what could happen to Dad. It would be unbearable to lose him.

Two Timers

I started out with the idea that kids find a device that lets them travel a short distance into either the past or the future. Time travel is very tricky to write about. (Note that I used "distance," which is a spatial measure, to talk about time in the first sentence. It is often easiest to think about time in terms of the properties of space.) When I realized I could set things up so someone traveled in both directions at once, I knew I had a solid basis for a story. As always, any given concept could have led me to all sorts of different endings. I'm not sure I should have let the bully win, and beat up the two kids. Maybe I'll travel back in time and tell myself to change this one so something bad happens to the bully. (Maybe I've already done that. You'll never know.)

Tanks for Your Contribution
I love visiting aquariums. Soon after I went to the amazing one in Boston, this idea came to me. I think it might actually have been inspired by the remoras, even though they don't suck blood, and by seeing signs for upcoming exhibits. I'll admit I thought about having the kid end up as fish food. And I'll bet some of you expected that, as you read the story. But I gave him a break.

The Girl Who Covered Her Face
The ending came from my "what if" file. The idea of unbearable beauty then led me to think about famous faces. After I seized on Helen of Troy, the rest fell right into place. It almost didn't make the collection. I wasn't sure whether the story was just a bit too dark and disturbing for a Weenies book, since there are many younger readers in my audience. (If you're one of my older readers, and able to handle disturbing stories, I put the tales that are definitely not suitable for the Weenies books into a collection called *Extremities: Stories of Death, Murder, and Revenge*.) I also contemplated an even darker ending, where she tries to destroy her face, but it didn't feel right.

Lucidity
Like Cole, I'd read an article about lucid dreaming. That gave me the basic idea for the story. I thought it would be fun to

write about a kid who gets obsessed with trying to know when he is dreaming. Unlike Cole, I don't have terrible friends who play pranks on me. But I have the sort of mind that thinks up pranks (even though I don't play them on my friends), so that gave me the idea for the ending. Speaking of which, the final line, where Benjie flies off (implying Cole is actually dreaming), was a last-minute addition. Until then, the story ended with the fairly weak and unsatisfying line, "Cole had a feeling the nightmare was just beginning." As I was looking for a better line about Cole, the idea to have Benjie fly off hit me. I hope that wasn't too much of a leap.

Bangs in Your Eyes

The beginning and the ending came to me pretty much together. (This is rare. If I know the opening, it usually takes a bit of thought, or a bit of writing, before I know the ending. And if I know the ending, I have to think a while before I know how things should start.) In this case, the idea of exploding faces and the actual explosion of the calculator arrived on the same bus.

The Talk

This story was born of my own hazy memories. I recall a day when the girls were called to the auditorium, to get a talk about things that applied only to them. I don't know if schools still do that. As I was putting together the collection, I was a bit worried that this story might be seen as implying that only the boys were lectured about becoming adults. That was definitely not my intention. For that matter, I have no idea what the girls in this story were told. And I'm happy to keep it that way.

Same Bird

My friend Josh, who likes to read my stories to his kids when they go camping, told me the following anecdote:

> *After reading your stories by the campfire, we all took a hike the following morning. My son kept finding feathers and collecting them, each time announcing "same bird." I said "This feels like a Weenies story. A boy is walking along finding feathers that he thinks are all from the same bird. As he continues, he finds a beak, a foot, etc. Eventually the bird reconstitutes in his hands and flies away." To which my daughter added, "But first he pecks out the boy's eyes."*

That's the sort of moment that would make any parent proud. Interestingly enough, I had an idea in my "what if" file about a kid on a hike who sees a dead bird, and then, a moment later, sees an identical one. But I liked this version better. As you can see, I gave it a slightly darker spin. I hope Avi and Isabel approve.

Haunting Your Thoughts

This came straight out of my files. "What if a house was haunted in a way where it did whatever each person living there feared the most?" (Some of my what-ifs are fairly long and rather specific, like this one, while others are a lot shorter.) I like to scatter classic horror forms throughout these books. I've written plenty of ghost stories, and I've touched on most of the other traditional monsters, as well. But a while back, I realized that I'd never written a haunted-house story. The what-if came to me when I was looking for an idea to fill this gap.

Differnet Explorer

Fairly often, when I try to type "different," I end up typing "differnet." The typo struck me as an interesting word. I realized it could mean a different type of Internet. Which led me to write about an Internet that is mostly far too familiar, but also different in one mind-numbing way that will make your head spin.

Healed

I'm not sure where the idea came from. I also wasn't sure whether to use the story. It's tricky writing about sick kids. But I've also heard from a lot of kids who've told me my stories helped them get through a tough time (as well as several adults who let me know they'd read my books while undergoing serious medical treatments), so I decided to take a chance.

Stunt Your Growth

When I see kids running around a mall, my first instinct is to trip them. I can't do that, of course. It would be wrong, and mean, and I'd get in trouble. But I can throw one of them down a cliff in a story. That feels even better.

Urban Girl

There are all sorts of urban legends and campfire stories about ghosts who appear to travelers and then disappear right after the traveler brings the ghost back home. I took that basic idea and combined it with the question, "what if an urban legend met another urban legend?" This is a very rich playing field for stories.

The Principle of Discipline

It is sometimes difficult for a school to get rid of a bully. Naturally, I thought about what would happen if a principal decided to make it easy to get rid of them. I'm often asked why I write about bullies. The answer is simple. Stories require conflict. (At least, the sort of stories I like to write.) Bullies are definitely a source of conflict. If you want to read a book that tells the story from the viewpoint of both the bullies and the victims, check out my novel *Flip*. It's a lot of fun.

Fwosty

As I look for new ideas for stories for these collections, I'm always searching for areas I haven't explored. I've written plenty of vampire stories, and I plan to write plenty more, because they are such a great subject, but I also like treading new ground. That's why, as I mentioned above, I wrote a haunted-house story. I was thinking about that one day, when I realized I wanted to write about a killer snowman. I might also have been influenced by those great Calvin and Hobbes snowman cartoons that are wonderfully dark and twisted.

Serves You Right

I guess I was looking at the children's items on a menu when this idea hit me. It's hard not to notice that kids usually get stuck with the same three or four things while the adults get tons of choices. I suspect the half-clever names they give those foods on the menu don't make them taste any better. And, in case you're wondering, I'm just as bad as the dad in the story. I don't like to stop once I'm on the road.

Blood Donors

In one of my first chapter books, *The Vanishing Vampire*, the main character discovers he not only can turn himself into a bat but he can also become a swarm of insects. I think this was on my mind when the idea for "Blood Donors" hit me. I like how this one starts out as one character's struggle but ends on a much larger scale.

Abra-ca-Deborah

As I mentioned earlier, I was a magic geek in my youth. I even participated in several competitions. I didn't win first place, but I guess the judges felt sorry for me because they gave me a special trophy for humor. Unfortunately, there is a bias in magic, as there is in many areas, against women. As the father of a brilliant and amazing daughter, I am a huge fan and supporter of talented young ladies. The original "what if" idea was "what if a witch had a passion for stage magic?" The idea to put her in a competition sprung naturally from that, given my own experiences.

The Quilty Clown

As I mentioned earlier, these Weenies collections give me great freedom to experiment in all sorts of ways. I decided it would be interesting to try to write a story from the viewpoint of an infant. As for the quilted clown, someone gave my daughter one when she was very little. (It went right into a closet.) And I know a lot of people find clowns scary or creepy. (I've explored this in other stories, such as "Mr. HooHaa!" from *The Curse of the Campfire Weenies*.) Making the viewpoint character so young was a great exercise. I felt the story was scary enough to earn the coveted position as the closer for the collection.

So, this is my eighth collection. The Weenies books, all together, contain more than 250 stories. Yikes. That's a lot. I feel extremely fortunate that I can share my stories with the world. I'm pretty sure there will be another collection or two (thanks to you, my readers, who've played a large part in making these books so popular). But I want to take my time, catch my breath, and give my inner artist a chance to daydream and dawdle. So it might be a while before you see number nine. Meanwhile, if you've read all eight Weenies collections and are eager for more of my work, please check out my other books. Some of them are also pretty warped and creepy.

READING AND ACTIVITY GUIDE

*Strikeout of the Bleacher Weenies and
Other Warped and Creepy Tales*

Ages 9–12; Grades 4–7

ABOUT THIS GUIDE

The questions and activities that follow are intended to enhance your reading of *Strikeout of the Bleacher Weenies*, the eighth book in David Lubar's popular anthology series. The guide has been developed in alignment with the Common Core State Standards; however, please feel free to adapt this content to suit the needs and interests of your students or reading group participants.

WRITING AND RESEARCH ACTIVITIES

I. Short Storytime

A. Go to the library or search online to find a definition of *short story* as a literary form.

(Hint: visit http://www.wwnorton.com/college/english/litweb10/glossary/S.aspx.) Make a list of authors considered to be masters of this genre. With friends or classmates, discuss favorite short stories you have read.

B. Start a reading journal for *Strikeout of the Bleacher Weenies*. For each story you read, use the journal to record some or all of the following:

- The main idea or concept of the story.
- A description of the main character.
- Favorite quotations.
- Situations in which the main character is in crisis and what advice readers might offer.
- New vocabulary words and/or a list of invented words.
- Sketches inspired by the novels.
- Questions readers would like to ask the author or characters from the novels.

II. Warped Wordplay and Paranormal Poetry

A. Go to the library or search online to find definitions for the following types of literary wordplay: Spoonerism, anagram, portmanteau word, and pun. Create a list or diagram of stories from the Bleacher Weenies collection that employ each of these types of wordplay.

B. The story "Parasites" begins with a real childhood rhyme which the author interprets in a creepy new way. Write down a familiar nursery rhyme, jump roping chant, or ditty sung to you by a parent or grandparent. Then, write 15–20 words or phrase expanding or reinterpreting this rhyme in a warped and creepy way.

C. In 1845, acclaimed writer of macabre poems and stories, Edgar Allan Poe, published one of his most famous works, "The Raven," which begins with the lines:

Once upon a midnight dreary, while I pondered, weak and weary,

Over many a quaint and curious volume of forgotten lore,
While I nodded, nearly napping, suddenly there came a
tapping,
As of some one gently rapping, rapping at my chamber door.

Use your imagination to write a creepy ending to this verse. Then, go to the library or search online to read Poe's finished poem.

(Hint: visit http://www.poemuseum.org/works-raven.php.) Compare Poe's first stanza with yours, and with the first stanzas completed by friends or classmates. Discuss how this exercise gives you insights into creativity and imagination.

D. "Dominant Species" is a story about sand, a seemingly dull topic. How does the author use wordplay to make dry scientific facts creepily exciting? Think of a word that seems boring to you. Try anagramming the word or employing another type of wordplay until you come up with an exciting way to write a short story on this topic. Write a paragraph describing your story.

E. Go to the library or search online to find a definition of the literary term *point of view* and its subcategories *limited*, *omniscient*, *first-person*, *second-person*, and *third-person*. What viewpoints does David Lubar use in the book? What types of narrators (adult, child, human, nonhuman) does he employ? Select one story from the collection and rewrite the first page from a different viewpoint than the one used by the author. Do you find this exercise easy or difficult? Write a short essay explaining why choosing the *point of view* is an important task for authors and why this might be particularly critical for writers of scary stories.

WRITING STORIES: THE BIGGER PICTURE

A. A feature that makes the Weenie anthologies special is the author's notes which follow the stories. David Lubar offers insights into his story inspirations and how he grows each idea into a complete tale. Among Lubar's favorite story starters are the words, "What if . . . ?" Make a list of 6–12 "What if" sentences of your own. Circle the two sentences you feel show the most potential for turning into a short story. If desired, write the complete story.

B. In his April 1848 essay for *Graham's Magazine*, "The Philosophy of Composition" (pp. 163–167), writer Edgar Allan Poe wrote: "There is a radical error, I think, in the usual mode of constructing a story . . . I prefer commencing with the consideration of an effect." Write a short essay explaining what you feel Poe means, and whether you believe David Lubar would agree or disagree with this statement and why.

C. In his afterword, David Lubar discusses the particular challenges of two stories: "Healed" ("It's tricky writing about sick kids") and "The Quilty Clown" ("Making the viewpoint character so young was a great exercise"). Write down several topics or viewpoints that might present particular writing challenges to you. Challenge yourself to write the opening paragraph for one of those stories.

D. Make a five-columned chart with the following headings: Supernatural; Dreams and Mind Games; Greed and Selfishness; Creepy Creatures; Parents and Kids. Write the title of each *Strikeout of the Bleacher Weenies* story in the column (or columns) that describe their key themes or features. Do most titles fall into one or into multiple categories? Do you think there should be additional columns in the chart and how might you title them? How does this exercise help you better understand David Lubar's process of creating a creepy story anthology?

E. David Lubar chose "Bleacher Weenies," but which story would you choose to headline this collection? Design a new cover for this Weenies book based on your selection. Would you also change the order of the stories? Write a short explanation for your choices. Include a revised table of contents noting your revised story organization. (Hint: If you have kept a reading journal per exercise 1.b, above, it might be a helpful reference.)

F. The story "Same Bird" was inspired by a story a friend told the author. Have you had a curious, funny, or scary experience that might make a fantastic story starter? Write a letter to David Lubar, describing your experience and why you think it might serve as inspiration for a story in a ninth Weenies collection.

Supports Common Core State Standards: W.4.1, 5.1, 6.1, 7.1; W.4.3, 5.3, 6.3, 7.3; SL.4.1, 5.1, 6.1, 7.1; SL.4.4, 5.4, 6.4, 7.4; RL.4.1–4, 5.1–4, 6.1–4, 7.1–4; RL. 4.6, 5.6, 6.6, 7.6.

QUESTIONS FOR DISCUSSION

1. *Strikeout of the Bleacher Weenies* is David Lubar's eighth Weenie story collection. Have you read other Lubar anthologies, or other story collections? Have you read other scary books? Did you begin reading this book with certain expectations? Explain your answer.

2. At the start of the first story, "Easy Targets," the narrator tells readers he wants to attend "PeaceJoy Charter

School." What assumptions might you make about the narrator based on the desire to attend a school with this name? What are the school and the narrator really like? In what ways does the structure and plot of this story prepare readers for the rest of this collection?

3. In "Swing Round," Sarah tells her friends, "It's okay to lie in the name of science." Is this true? Do you think the author is making a larger point about scientific behaviors in the real world? In what other stories do a lack of research, ill-preparedness or idle curiosity cause scary results?

4. "Frozen in Time" and "Two Timers" are time-travel tales. Compare and contrast these stories in terms of the method of time travel, the characters' attitudes toward being able to time travel, and the results of their time-travel journey. Would you like to try time travel? Why or why not?

5. In "A Word or Two About These Stories" at the back of the book, David Lubar admits to being a "magic geek" as a kid. Do you think this admission adds insight into your reading of "All the Tricks" and "Abra-ca-Deborah"? Do you have a hobby or special interest about which you would like to write a short story? What element of your obsession would you be certain to include in your tale?

6. "EnDANGERed" and "Urban Girl" feature supernatural characters. In what ways does the author challenge traditional views of demons? Are the demons in these stories good or bad?

7. "Strikeout of the Bleacher Weenies" pokes some creepy fun at over-obsessed sports parents. What other stories in the collection feature indulgent, weak or angry parents? How are the kid narrators of these stories affected by their parents' imperfections? Why do you think the author chose this story with which to title this collection?

8. "The Principle of Discipline" offers a scary and thought-provoking perspective on the issue of bullies. Do you think the narrator's fate was fair or unfair? Has this story, along with the story "Easy Targets," affected your thoughts about the issue of bullies? Explain your answer.

9. Throughout the collection, many characters come to bad ends as a result of their own greed, laziness, and lies. Could you argue that "Bangs in Your Eyes" is the story that best exemplifies this phenomenon? Do you think that this story collection can be read as a warning against selfishness? Explain your answers.

Supports Common Core State Standards: RL.4.1–4, 5.1–4, 6.1–4, 7.1–4; RL. 4.6, 5.6, 6.6, 7.6; SL.4.1, 5.1, 6.1, 7.1; SL.4.4, 5.4, 6.4, 7.4.

ABOUT THE AUTHOR

David Lubar grew up in Morristown, New Jersey. His books include the acclaimed novels *Hidden Talents*, *True Talents*, and *Flip*; the popular Nathan Abercrombie, Accidental Zombie series; and the bestselling Weenies short-story collections. He lives in Nazareth, Pennsylvania. You can visit him on the Web at www.davidlubar.com.